The Emergence of a Legend

'Be Strong'

Manny Twofeathers

MANNY TWOFEATHERS

6/1/04

X

Wo-Pila Publishing
Erie, Pennsylvania

First Printing: May, 2004

This novel is a work of fiction. Names, characters, places, and incidents either are the product of the author's imagination or are used fictitiously. Any resemblance to actual persons, living or dead, events or locales is entirely coincidental. It is not intended in any way to be of historical fact, and should not be used as reference material in any way.

Library of Congress Control Number: 2003114630

Twofeathers, Manny
    Kokopelli's Dream

ISBN: 1-886340-23-4

Cover design: Manny Twofeathers

TABLE OF CONTENTS

ACKNOWLEDGEMENTS

I want to thank the Spirit of Kokopelli for choosing me to be the one to tell his story and pushing me to finish this book. I also want to thank my good friends Bob Dieleman and his wife Kay, his sister Kathy, and mother Ruth Dieleman for their help, support and believing in me. To Sandra Sax for consulting on the book design. Special thanks to friends Barb & Doug Greiner from Turquoise Spirit for helping to make this book possible, and Marlene O'Connor for being there for us all these years. I also want to honor my children, Stone and Oriona for putting up with me, and my mother-in-law, Lynne Babuin for all her help, love, and support.

Last, but not least, for she is my rock and anchor, my wife Melody (formerly Betty Hutton), for <u>not</u> helping me write and forcing me to look deep within myself for the story that had to be told. For all her love, patience, editing and the hardest part of writing - making all my mistakes be right. I am most grateful.

INTRODUCTION

Who was Kokopelli?

Where did he come from? No one knows for sure. In all the research, my wife Melody and I have done and all the stories I have heard, he exists only as a full-grown adult. No place of origin was ever mentioned.

Why did he become so popular and well known? I believe everyone he touched during his life liked and respected Kokopelli, regardless of how short or long it might have been.

What was the reason he appeared?

Was he just a common man who loved to live life to the fullest?

Some stories make him seem to be a holy man. Others tell of him being the bringer of babies and a scoundrel. Others give his image the power of bringing creativity and sexuality to those who believed in him.

He certainly left an impression on many people in the distant past, and he is most certainly making an impression on many of us today. Does he really help us when we ask or believe in him?

You may hear many different stories about where he came from and his exploits. Of course, everyone wants to lay claim to this colorful character that lived so long ago.

Of all the millions of people who have been born, lived, and died here in Aztlan (America), how many of them are still remembered? How many other people's likenesses have been carved in stone? Montezuma the Great Chief of the Mexica (Aztecs) is remembered in history books. Some of the old Mexica (Aztec) gods were also carved in stone.

Many nations such as the Incas, the Aztecs, the Mayans, and the Toltecs are remembered as great nations and cultures. The cliff dwellers of North America have left their legacy behind for us to remember them by.

Then here we have a flute player, Kokopelli that was supposed to have been an actual living man. Why is he, above most other individuals, still remembered? Is he or has he always been just a belief? Kokopelli's likeness was carved in stone, why did the old people do this. Why did they want us to know about him in the future? They knew we would see their work, be curious and wonder about him. Did they believe he could help us if we remembered him and what he stood for?

To me, he has been a focus point where I have found inspiration and even hope. In fact, this book was inspired by a dream I had about Kokopelli. My dream told me to write about him, and that I was to walk in his sandals and see his world through my eyes. In my dream, to whomever I was talking to, I said I knew nothing about Kokopelli. So how could I write about him? I clearly received the message not to worry - to just write, and what I needed to write would come to me. All I can do is write and call it fiction - or is it?

I use many Spanish words to make it easier for me to write this book. It is a language I speak and understand. Some of the words are considered Spanish or Mexican but are in fact ancient words from some of the old people.

As Kokopelli walks through on this journey, he will in fact cross from one era in time to another without him being aware that it has happened. He travels through the times of the height of Mayan power to the times of the later arrivals, the Mexica people.

Always keep in mind that this is not a history book and only a story. It is not meant to be used, in any way, for reference or referred to for historical or research purposes. However, the lessons he brings in this book can be used to better your life.

There were a couple of interesting bits of information brought to my attention while I was writing this book. Researching on the Internet for information on my daughter, Oriona's school project, Melody typed in "Religious Symbols" and to our astonishment, Kokopelli's figure was on the list. This demonstrates the impact he has left behind.

So here is my fictional story about a character I find very fascinating. Kokopelli has inspired me many times. His unknown origin and the stories of his life have intrigued me for many years. This book is truly a tribute to him and his image, whether he actually lived or not. It is based on some stories I have heard about him, mixed with my own dreams, and spiritually inspired words, of what may have happened so long ago. Join me as we travel through the life of an extraordinary Man, Spirit or both.

CHAPTER 1

MY DREAM BEGINS

Last night I stopped in a village. I had been traveling on foot for several suns from the last village where they treated me very well. The elders from the village last night asked me to eat and visit with them so I could tell them the stories from other more distant villages and nations. I did not understand my reluctance to spend the night or why I refused their kindness. I felt something urgent pushing me to go on my way. Perhaps I was being pushed to reach the end of this trail or was needed elsewhere for something important. I guess I was where I was supposed to be for whatever reason.

After I left the village last night, I was having difficulty staying on the trail. My eyes are not too good anymore and the only light I had was from the stars. Since the stars were covered with clouds, I now wished I had remained in the village.

Not being able to see very well, I strayed off the trail. In my old clumsiness, I lost my footing and fell what seemed to be a short distance. I landed hard and I thought my hip was broke. There is also something wrong with my back. In the right side of my chest, I feel a terrible pain. It might be that one of my ribs has broken. I realize that I am not in very good shape, but I will pull through this. All I need is a little help.

I play a few notes on my flute, then stop, and listen. Nothing! The only sound is the light rustling of a breeze through the short sage bushes and an occasional exploring mouse. There are two crickets talking back and forth to each other until they get tired and eventually stop.

I have now been lying here a while and some of the pain seems to have subsided. I try to move and cannot. I can stand the pain, but have very little feeling in my legs. Resigned to my situation, I lay still and wait for someone to find me. When the night passes perhaps, I can attract a passerby's attention by playing my flute.

One by one I see all my celestial brothers, pass over me. The moon comes up but it is only a sliver, it is almost upside down. Somewhere back in my life, someone told me that when the moon is like that, it would not hold anything, even pity. The constellation Orion slowly marches across the sky. The Lion and the Ram also take their turn crossing from horizon to horizon. The Big and the Little Dippers appear and slowly reach their zenith then drop to the western horizon.

While I lay there, I am listening for my rescuers. Many people should be traveling this trail, so all I have to do is be patient and they will come. I have to believe that.

If I can play my flute for just a little while perhaps I will feel better. I try but find it difficult to put the flute to my lips. I cannot do such a simple little thing as that. I have failed. It is better to save my strength for when I hear people passing by. I blame my inability to move on the position in which I am laying.

I now have the chance to think. As I lay there, I begin to think of my past and all the things I have done, the places I have been and the people that I have met. Though I am not in so much pain now, I feel tired. I feel myself slowly drifting, drifting, my eyelids getting heavy. My body is relaxing even though my mind still works. I feel myself sliding into that comfortable place of rest. I remember one last thought, "Sleep, you need the rest. Tomorrow you will be found and you will need the strength," I say to myself.

Finally, my eyelids close and I sleep and I Dream . . .

CHAPTER 2

A NEW WORLD, ANOTHER JOURNEY

One second I was not, the next second I was!

I found myself walking through dense foliage. It was very warm and humid. As I walked, I soon felt sweat beading on my forehead and upper lip under my mustache. I felt the rest of my face and realized that I also had a full beard. It was light brown in color. I stood as high as the neck of a tall horse with its head up. My hands and arms were brown and strong. I walked with strength in my legs and with a good long stride.

I was carrying a beautiful wooden flute in my hands. I put it to my lips and blew on it softly. I was surprised at how soothing and beautiful the notes were and that I was the one making them. I seemed to recall sitting on a rock and playing my flute to a large flock of sheep, to calm them and get them to bed down at nightfall. The flute I found in my hands was not the same one I had before. I cannot recall where or how I came to be in possession of this one! Strange! Things are strange for me indeed.

I felt confused. I tried to recall where I was coming from and where it is that I am going and why.

From somewhere in the back of my mind, I seemed to recall one or was it two brothers and someone else, an older man. Was he my father? I felt a deep love for them. I longed for them yet never could recall much about them. I felt emptiness inside and did not understand why it was so.

I also missed the country where I grew into a man. Nothing was clear - it all seemed a foggy memory. Those thoughts brought emptiness into my heart. In my memory, I could see a beautiful desert country, one without as much vegetation as here. I remembered a harsh but beautiful land of dry heat, rocks, and very sparse vegetation growth.

I walked on, my strides long and strong, as though on a mission or an important quest.

The heavy growth of trees and bushes dripped with humidity and heavy moisture. The vegetation seemed to be trying to hide the trail where I was walking. I saw signs of where humans had cut the brush away, trying to keep the trail clear. From this I knew there were people not far from where I was walking. I felt the intense heat and knew I had not been in this country very long and I was not accustomed to it.

Even the scents of this country were different and strange to me. As I walked, the smells changed from rotting vegetation to overripe fruit on the ground. Then it changed to the sweet smell of a large variety of blooming flowers.

4

Some were large and purple. Other flowers were also large but red. Then some were small and yellow, but all of them released their beautiful smells, trying to attract the attention of the bees and hummingbirds. Even the Standing People knew they needed the winged ones to pollinate each other. Therefore, they attract them with sweet smells and sweeter nectar. We can learn something from the birds and the bees. It is much easier to catch friends with love and kindness than with anger and bitterness.

I was wearing a long, white hand woven heavy robe, with a piece of the same cloth, wrapped around my head. The heat under the heavy cloth was rapidly becoming almost unbearable. I removed the cloth tie that was around my waist and opened my robe. I found that I was totally nude underneath the robe. I knew that I would have to be careful when I encountered others. They might think badly of me if my privates and manhood were exposed to the world. I removed my head wrap and tossed it over my shoulder. Once free, my hair fell loosely over my shoulders. The breeze that touched my scalp beneath my hair felt wonderful.

I put my flute to my lips, raised my face to the heavens, and started a song of loneliness from my heart. The first notes were low, soft, and mournful. I played as I walked. As my heart received happiness from the notes, my step quickened, as did my heart. I thought that even though I was lonesome, I was alive and well. It felt good to be this way.

Hunger and thirst were beginning to let me know it had been awhile since I had eaten. I thought about it and could not recall when I had in fact eaten last. I did not recall when

I had started my fast, but now I was looking forward to breaking it.

Ahead of me, just off the trail, I could see in a tree a beautiful blue long tailed bird. It was standing on one leg, its talons grasping a tree branch to hang on, as the other talon held a piece of ripe yellow oblong fruit. With its powerful beak, it tore off pieces as it ate. It must have tasted good, for it ignored me until I got close. When I was very close, the bird with the beautiful blue feathers stopped, looked at me, cocked its head to one side, and gave me a challenging look. It was a brave and feisty bird; I liked that in a person or animal. It squawked loudly, attempting to scare me off. When I did not stop, it screamed once more as loud as it could, dropped the fruit, and flew off.

The fruit dropped on the ground in front of me. I picked it up and smelled it. It had a pleasant but strange smell. I extended my tongue and savored the fruit. The taste was also strange to me. I had never tasted such a sweet and delicious fruit in my life.

It was so delicious and moist I can still taste it. Perhaps my hunger had something to do with how good it tasted and smelled. I ate the fruit with more confidence. I thought if the bird could eat it without a problem, I should be able to eat it.

As I stood there and ate, I looked around. I noticed the insects and heard many different sounds. Somewhere deep in the forest I heard the screams of what I believed were other kinds of birds. A pair of bright green birds flew over me. Within the trees and brush around me, I saw small, blue, red, and yellow birds. They reminded me of the flowers. 'Flowers in flight', I thought and chuckled to myself. I also hear what I believe is the cough of a large Jaguar or cougar. I thought this was where a person had to stay alert and awake.

Slowly my hunger faded away. After I finished eating, I wiped the fruit juice from my mouth and mustache with the edge of my robe. Though I was not full, my hunger was gone. I remembered that it is good to eat only in moderation. That always helps the body to stay healthy and the mind alert. Not wanting to get overly full, I decided not to have any more, even as good as it was.

There were many pieces of fruit hanging on the tree. I decided to take a few with me to eat later in the day, when I would surely get hungry. By stretching, I could reach some of the fruit on the lower branches. I selected three pieces that looked good to me. Because it was so plentiful, I was tempted to eat one more. Again, I reminded myself of the consequences of overeating.

I tied the three pieces of fruit in my head wrap, tied the ends together, and put it across my back. That way it left my hands free to carry or play my flute as I walked.

I continued on my way, wherever it was that I was going. As I walked, my eyes were busy looking here, looking there, marveling at all the new and strange things that were unfolding before my very eyes. My senses were reeling. Everything I saw, smelled, or felt was very strange to me. I wondered where I was and why I had come here. I wondered who brought me here and why. Questions and more questions but where could I find the answers?

As I walked through the heavy foliage, I realized the trail was getting wider and showed signs of heavier use, meaning that I was getting closer to a town, village or at least someone's home.

I had been walking long enough to begin to grow weary. My feet were telling me to sit a while and remove my sandals. They were my transportation and needed my care.

Next to the trail was a large fallen tree. I noticed other weary travelers had also found it a convenient place to rest in the past. Before I sat, I stood there in wonder at the size, length, and girth of this beautiful tree. It must have been a wonder even amongst its own kind. What a beautiful specimen of the Standing People to have grown to such huge proportions, I thought to myself. I marveled at it again. I do not believe I ever saw a tree as large as this one. The beautiful things I saw made me think of God and all that He creates for us to look upon and use.

I tried to think of all the things we get from trees, such as lumber to build homes, boats, large ships and wood to heat our homes. Trees also give us shade to rest under on a hot summer day, and fruit to eat. Trees give beauty to our world. For one moment, can you imagine what our world would look like without trees? I do not know how, but deep inside I feel in some way they help give us life itself. There must be a more important reason why we respect the Standing People, other than just wood, shade, and fruit. I often wondered why we hold trees in such high esteem.

It was too high to sit on top of it, so I did as others had done. I sat on the ground next to it and leaned my tired back on it. A long contented sigh escaped my mouth. It felt so good to stop and just relax for a moment.

I felt my legs relaxing and my feet tingled from the walk. I reached down and removed my leather sandals.

They were so soft and light that I hardly noticed them, but it still felt good to take them off my feet for a little while. As I looked around, I slowly massaged first my right then my left foot. It felt good.

As I worked on my feet with my thumbs, I looked for and found the points on my feet that corresponded with the different parts of my body. That way I was able to work on my back, my head, and different internal organs. I do not recall who taught me to do this, but I feel as though I have always done it. I remembered someone telling me if I used a few moments to care for myself this way, I would seldom need a person of medicine, if ever. I would become my own healer. This was important for me, as I was always on the trail to places unknown and worse still, facing the unexpected on a daily basis. Places to get medicine or the healers to give it were rare.

I finished working on my feet and pulled my sandals back on. Still sitting and relaxing I put the flute to my lips. I blew softly, using only my exhaled breath to coax music from it. It brought happiness to my heart. The foliage around me seemed to stop to listen. The slight breeze also paused to hear what I was saying with the flute.

The birds grew quiet as though listening. They must have wondered if the sounds came from some new kind of bird. The sounds were pleasant but they were strange calls.

As I played, I noticed a deer doe walk up slowly. She stopped close to where I was sitting. She looked around, making sure she was alone with this strange creature and listened. She seemed to be full of curiosity. When I finished playing, the spell was broken. The breeze started whispering again, the birds went on with their chirping and the deer walked on without fear.

Refreshed and rejuvenated, I continued on my way. I did not know the reason, but I felt an urgency and quickened my step. I felt as though some important thing awaited me. My strength helped me as I lengthened my stride.

To the best of my knowledge, I was either twenty-two or twenty-three summers when this life began. I was no longer a very young man, but I was still strong. Back then, most men lived until thirty five to forty five summers, and this was considered old age. If a person, man, or woman, lived beyond fifty summers, they were considered ancient and elders of the most respectable kind.

The shadows were starting to lengthen. The sun had long, passed its zenith, and was on its way to sleep. The day was almost at an end. Just as I began to wonder and look for a place I might sleep, I started to hear noises not too far ahead of me. The noise was like people yelling and dogs barking. I was glad to know there was a village ahead. It would be a place to eat, sleep, and rest. It never crossed my mind that I might not be welcomed and treated with respect. I did not know where such confidence came from, but I accepted it. That was the way it had always been for me.

As I got closer, I heard the harsh sounds much better. Not knowing what the yelling was about, I wondered what it might mean. The voices I could not hear clearly but were angry and loud, that much I could tell. It took me a few minutes to hear what was being said. I was surprised that I could understand what was being said. They were words of hate and asking that someone's life be taken.

As I walked out of the dense undergrowth and trees, a few people and a small group of dogs and children saw me. The children began to yell and the dogs barked.

CHAPTER 3

FIRST ENCOUNTER

Faced with a situation I had not experienced before, I was startled for a moment, but I kept on walking. To overcome my surprise, I put my flute to my lips and started to play. The sound of my flute slowly began to reach the angry people. I played a soothing heart song for them. One by one, people stopped yelling and turned around to look my way. They seemed surprised at my appearance as I continued walking toward them.

Even the dogs stopped barking and followed me; wagging their tails, looking at the villagers as though saying, look what we have found!

As I walked playing my flute, the crowd of people parted before me. I arrived where there was space around several elders. I assumed they were leaders and stopped before them.

I stopped playing and gave them my most majestic and deepest bow I could muster. Bending at the waist, my head went as low as my knees. In this way, I was showing them the greatest respect.

The men and almost everyone else were of a dark cinnamon color, with nice clear skin. They were a handsome people. None of the men I saw had any facial hair. In general, their bodies were slender. My light skin, light brown hair, full beard, and mustache made me stand out like a sore red nose.

Pulling my scarf off my shoulders, I unwrapped the fruit I had picked earlier. For a moment, as I pulled the scarf off, I saw a bit of apprehension cross their faces, until they realized that I meant no harm to them. I honored each of them with a piece of fruit.

First, I stepped up to the taller thin man and offered him the fruit, assuming he was the leader or chief. He bowed his head ever so slightly, enough that everyone saw him accept my offering. I was right. The others backed up respectfully to let him be in the front and center.

The Grand Chief was wearing a long loincloth that reached almost to the ground in front and behind him. His white robe was tied over his left shoulder and was under his right arm, leaving his arm free to be used for whatever was needed. The material was beautifully decorated with a thin gold thread trim that set him apart from the others.

The other elders wore the same kind of robes of different colors, except theirs were tied over the right shoulder. This was their way to show respect for the leader. They were willing to cover their right arm to hamper movement of that arm, and therefore, be less threatening to their Chief.

The majority of all the other people wore only loincloths and some had on short vests. They also dyed their loin clothes in many different colors.

Then I handed one of the fruits to the shorter fat man. He grunted. I took it to be a thank you or just recognition of the gift. I think he did it only because their leader had acknowledged me. Then I handed one to the last and older of the three. He accepted his with very little interest, as though he had just had one for lunch.

It was all I had to offer, but food represents life and they accepted it. They could see I was a poor and simple man and all I had was my clothes, flute, and the fruit I offered.

Somewhere along the trail, I was advised to never visit a person's home without bearing at least one gift. The fruit had been my gift to their home. I believe they were impressed that, as poor as I appeared to be, I was still willing to give the little I had. That went well toward breaking the tension for everyone.

Behind the elders was a magnificently built enormous stone pyramid. I noticed as I stood waiting for someone to speak, that there were several men putting torches to upright metal urns. They were lighting them to create light, for full darkness had fallen. On top of the pyramid, I saw another man wearing a large headdress with long feathers, also lighting four urns. The fire lit up the top of the pyramid as if it were day.

Off to one side was a large clay pot. Clouds of smoke rose from it and drifted down to ground level. It was a beautiful smell. It drifted throughout the entire area around the base of the pyramid. Later I found out that it was sacred and called Copal. Copal was a tree sap used by spiritual

13

people in different parts of this world. The way Copal was being used must mean it was readily available.

I looked back at the elders with a question on my face. There were three men wearing only loincloths kneeling on the cobble brick in front of them, their foreheads touching the ground and their hands tied behind them. I could not see their faces. The feeling of dread was in the air. One of them shivered for a moment, then stopped. They might be prisoners but they were also brave men. Their manly pride would not allow them to beg or plead for their lives.

Around the circle of people, there were several young men. All of them carried long wooden lances with long, sharp obsidian stone points at the end. They looked very lethal.

Another tall, thin and dark elder, with his robe tied over his right shoulder, stepped forward toward me and asked who I was and why I walked in and disrupted the court.

I quickly learned that men with robes over their loincloths were men of importance, but only the Grand Chief wore the robe tied over his left shoulder.

The tall, thin nobleman was not one of the three I had honored. He seemed to be a little angry. He stood in front of me with his hands on his hips, waiting for my answer.

I had been looking all around, but as he addressed me, I looked straight at him and explained that I was a stranger, a traveler, and bringer of gifts. The gifts I brought were of wisdom and knowledge.

"What wisdom might one as young as you bring to us elders that have lived so much longer?" he asked.

"I brought the wisdom of distance and knowledge of far off lands. By no means do I dare to presume I might possess more wisdom than any of you, for you are my elders."

I told them I had traveled to many different and strange lands in my young life. I had been very fortunate to encounter many men of wisdom such as them, I explained, loud enough so everyone could hear me.

To my surprise, I could understand what they were saying. I could not start to imagine how I had acquired the ability to speak their language. It was frightening to me, but only because I did not understand how or why this had happened to me. Another thing that surprised me was that I was such an eloquent speaker. It appeared they also recognized it and therefore accepted the fact that I was a person worth listening to, and a man with more than just a passable education.

I did know this was not my mother language, yet I could understand everything said. In addition, I could not remember the language I had spoken before I arrived at this place. Somewhere in the recesses of my mind, I recalled a word "Aramaic." Was that the name of my people or the name of my language or was it both? I could not recall where I had learned to speak as I was doing now.

For me it was difficult. All I had to depend on were things ingrained in my brain through upbringing. The good manners I had were also things I learned in my childhood. One other thing happened to me that helped channel my new life. It was the visions and dreams of things that happened to me in the past. I would see them either in my sleep or in my mind's eye while awake. Now I was beginning to understand the old visions and dreams.

The shortest of the three elders stepped toward me. He was still holding the fruit I gave him. He said to the others, his voice pleasant-sounding but hard, that perhaps I had come to try to trick them and help these prisoners escape.

He was short and heavyset. His hair was long on the back of his head and, despite his age, it was still black. The front of his head was quite bald. His eyes were close together and were full of meanness. He reminded me of a small swine.

I told them I could not have come to help them escape, for I did not know them or anything about them. I had brought knowledge from another world, far from this beautiful place where they lived.

I knew if I did not make myself clear quickly; I could find myself in bad trouble. I went on speaking but directed my attention to the Grand Chief and principal elder.

I said without emotion, that I did not know the men nor did I know what their crime was. Nor did I know what their punishment would be. I would not interfere in what they were doing. I had still been looking around the circle of men as I said that, as if I had any power to change the outcome of anything that happened here! Once again, as I was talking I turned and addressed my answer to the Grand Chief. I did not want the short fat elder to think I was obligated to answer to him personally. To myself I thought I did not want to end up kneeling next to the three men on the ground!

The first elder seemed to be the one with the most power. He said they were captured enemy warriors and the Medicine Priests said they must die.

He said they had to be sacrificed to the gods in order to bring prosperity and more children to their people. Their numbers seemed to have declined the last few summers.

"Why must they die?" I asked, not wanting to get involved, yet not being able to stop my question.

The Grand Chief replied, "We have always done it this way. They do the same to us. We must always have sacrifices and offer human blood to the Spirits. It is better to use enemies blood rather than our own people's blood."

I looked deep into the Grand Chief's eyes and he looked into mine. There seemed to be recognition between us, of two spiritual men – each with our own path. The Grand Chief said to me that he felt I must have a great deal of courage to come into their circle the way I had. He also said he respected me for my boldness. In turn, I said to the Grand Chief that I had seen in my mind's eye that he was a man of great compassion and had a willingness to learn. We understood one another and felt a mutual respect and liking for each other.

To change the energy and the way the conversation was going, I asked them what their people were called. I hoped they would not notice my evasiveness.

"We are Mayas, and our land is called Yucatan," exclaimed a couple of the elders, with pride in their voices. Then one of the two told me, with a note of even more pride, that their city was called the pearl of Yucatan, Chi-Chen Itza and that it was the largest and most beautiful city in all the world of Aztlan.

I asked where Aztlan was, and one of them said that the land of Aztlan extended many moons of travel to the north all the way, where the land was covered with ice.

17

I told them I was surprised that I had not heard of such a great people, but I had come from far off lands and had many things yet to learn.

I could not answer their question about where I had come from or where I was going. I was not sure of the answer myself. In all honesty, I could not tell the truth because I did not know what the truth was. I felt as though I was a spirit traveling through space, without substance.

"Where are these far lands you speak of?" asked the Grand Chief.

As I pointed away from the setting Sun to the East I said, "From where we now stand, I came from there. My lands are far off to the east where the sun awakens every morning."

I told them I could not explain how I had come to be in their country, for only God and the Spirits knew how I traveled and why. I do know that I was sent by the Great Spirit to bring love, happiness, understanding, and compassion to the people I encounter.

He then asked me if I owned the lands, I spoke about.

"No, I am but a poor traveler who only walks on the land."

The Grand Chief asked me what I was called. I replied that where I had come from, I was called, "One that walks with Spirits."

"One that walks with Spirits," . . . "Ho! It is good. That is a strong and special name," the Grand Chief said. "To us you would be 'Spirit Walker' and in our tongue it would be Koko-pelli. As long as you are with us, we will use the name Koko-pelli for you. It is easier for us to say it and remember."

It sounded like a good name. I could not remember what I was called before I arrived in this new world.

Behind me, I could hear the crowd whispering the name, "Kokopelli," "Kokopelli," as though they wanted to be sure that they could remember it. I liked it for it had a good sound to it. Still it surprised me because I could not understand why they thought my new name was important. I was flattered, but it embarrassed me.

I put the flute to my lips and commenced playing. Many thought I did this to entertain them, but in truth, it gave me a chance to think or dodge uncomfortable questions and overcome my embarrassment. Once again, everyone stopped talking to listen to me play.

When my notes reached the top of the pyramid, it seemed to touch the High Priest. He was on top waiting for the prisoners to be brought to him. He made a motion of recognition with his arms, walked to the back of the pyramid, and disappeared. I found him later to be a fine and considerate man, but with strong traditional beliefs. His name was Media Luna (Half Moon) whose beliefs included taking the lives of enemies.

He practiced sacrificing enemies to the Gods in what they considered a very humane way – by bloodletting. In a human sacrifice, a vein is cut and the victim slowly bleeds to death. He would lose blood and finally pass out and die in an unconscious state.

The short heavy set older man, had grown irritated, stepped forward and said he had heard enough of my flute playing. They needed to get on with the bloodletting.

I stopped playing.

Several men moved forward to grab the prisoners. The Grand Chief called to them in a loud voice. Everyone looked as though they had run into a wall and stopped. As they all grew quiet, he announced that it was getting late. He was hungry and wanted to hear what I had to say. He did not want to hear anything new or different while having to listen to his stomach growling at him for not tending to his hunger.

As if by magic, the prisoners were walked off. As they were led away, the prisoners turned and gave me a look of gratitude and they wondered how I had the power to stop their execution. One of them said my new name, "Kokopelli" (I could see his lips move); he raised one hand in a salute as he said it.

CHAPTER 4

FIRST FEAST

The crowd dispersed and the Grand Chief led me and two elders to a stone house some distance away from the pyramid. Many others with robes on their shoulders followed, making sure to remain well behind us.

As we walked, several things came to mind. First, I realized I was walking among people who were very intelligent and advanced in science, astronomy, and metallurgy. I had noticed this in the brief period I had been there. Another thing I realized was that they had some very cruel ways about them. I would call it lack of compassion. I knew this must be their custom. To them it was not cruel but the accepted way of life. They might not know any other way.

After we were inside the large building, the Grand Chief motioned for all of us to sit. It was hot and humid inside, but it looked as though I was the only one that noticed it. Everyone else seemed quite comfortable.

There must have been at least twenty people there, all men. I think most had followed because of their curiosity about me, the stranger. Women were only there to serve the food.

The floor and even the pillows were covered with many different animal hides. Most of them I did not recognize but I could see cougar, panther, deer and several large brown hides on the floor.

The floor itself was beautifully cut and fitted with stone tiles. The artisans had made large designs of celestial configurations. The sun, moon, and stars intertwined with pictures of men and beasts. It was done beautifully.

Everyone made themselves comfortable on large wooden hand-hewn benches. The benches were placed around a long, thick-topped wooden table. There was one beautiful chair at the head of the table. No one sat in it. Everyone knew it was for the Grand Chief. He walked to it and sat down.

Attractive dark skinned women dressed in light, white, full length dresses brought in several large platters of broiled meat. They were placed in different places on the large long table.

Other dishes were some I have never seen before. One I did recognize was boiled squash with onions. Another was an oblong green vegetable that when skinned, had small, yellow rows of grain that resembled teeth. This was very good and called elotes (corn).

They brought in three bowls overflowing with fresh small dark green vegetables with a small curved stem (jalapenos), which I never saw before. They must be good, for everyone immediately grabbed one or two of them.

I followed their example and took one. I did not want to appear ignorant, so I waited to see what they did before I did something foolish. The other bowl was filled to the top with small round dried red pieces of another vegetable (chili tepines). These must not have been as good, for only a few men asked for the bowl to be passed to them, and they took them very sparingly.

One woman brought a large stack of small round flat pieces of bread (corn tortillas). She put them on pieces of cloth in small stacks close to all of us. They brought in two large clay pots with a bright red chili sauce and meat (red chili con carne) in them. In two larger clay pots was a brown food (pinto beans or frijoles) and the other had small black beans. They were still hot and steaming.

To drink, they brought in a white drink fermented from corn that was alcoholic (pulque). Another alcoholic drink they brought in was a clear liquid made from a large desert cactus plant. The drink was called Mescal. The girl that brought it in told me if I drank some to be careful, as it was strong and made people drunk. She also told me it was used to start fires. In several other clay pitchers, there was a hot steaming dark brown liquid (chocolate) that was delicious, sweet, and tasty.

Then one of the young women brought in a white metal pot of a steaming hot and very good smelling beverage. She asked me, as she put a clay cup next to me if I wanted some café (coffee). I replied that I did not know what it was. Another girl was carrying a couple of other containers, one with milk, and one with honey. She poured the cup full of coffee then poured in the milk; I found out later it was goats' milk. Then she poured honey into it. Using my knife, she stirred it for me. She handed me the cup and stood looking and waiting for me to taste it. Lifting the cup to my lips I had to blow on it, it was very hot. I sipped at the edge of the cup pulling in the hot liquid. It was one of the most wonderful beverages I had ever tasted. Smiling, I drank more of it. She smiled too and satisfied that I liked it she moved on pouring coffee for others around the table.

There was a strong smell of onions, garlic, oregano, and other spices. It made the whole room smell aromatic. My stomach growled loudly with anticipation of receiving the food that was so close.

A beautiful young woman filled a flat clay plate with generous helpings of both the red sauce and the brown beans. The red sauce had chunks of meat in the sauce. I asked and was told it was deer meat.

Everyone was served but no one started eating. They were all looking at me. I bowed my head and said a short prayer. They all looked at me curiously wondering what I was doing. With a wooden spoon, I picked up a piece of meat covered with the red sauce and put it in my mouth. The first initial taste was wonderful. I smiled and nodded my approval. Everyone smiled in return with grunts of satisfaction and commenced eating.

Then it hit me. From a smooth, mellow spicy taste - to one that set my mouth on fire! I chewed the meat, swallowed quickly, coughed, and started gasping for air. I felt like a fish out of water. At first, I thought they were laughing at me. However, I also saw, between my coughing, they were all eating the same thing as I. It did not seem to be affecting them as it did me. I picked up a clay pitcher of water and almost emptied it.

Sweat started pouring off my forehead and saliva was dripping out of my mouth. Many turned to look at me. They did not understand why I behaved this way. I never felt such pain and agony. Tears ran down my cheeks. I looked wildly from person to person. I must have looked very amusing to them in this condition.

One of them tried to suppress a laugh and covered his mouth. Another person saw him and could not stop his laugh. Then from one person to another the laughter spread throughout the room. People would look at me spitting and gasping and laugh even harder. After a few moments, the laughter started to subside. My host also laughed, and then said, that was enough of the laughter. They did not want their new guest to think this was done intentionally.

Looking at everyone else in the entire hall, I wanted to know why they had given me fire. My pained gaze took in everyone as I looked back and forth. "We have done nothing to you," one man assured me. "This is how we always eat."

"Have you not ever eaten nor tasted chilies before?" asked another. My mouth was burning so much that I could not answer. All I did was shake my head.

If I ate some beans (frijoles) with the chili meat and if I drank some of the hot Café or chocolate it would stop burning. He said it would be uncomfortable for a few moments but then it would quit hurting. Another man pointed at the small brown beans lying in their own thick brown juice. Then with a piece of tortilla he showed me how to make it into a small scoop, fill it with frijoles, and eat the whole thing. I tried it and it worked. The burning in my mouth slowly started to go away as I ate more of the beans. I stayed away from the hot chili sauce!

As I watched them, they would fill their piece of tortilla with beans, put it in their mouth, and then take a bite of the small green vegetable. Then they would talk and laugh with their mouths full chew and swallow. Some of them would lay the tortilla on the palm of their hand, and with the other

25

hand roll the tortilla into a little roll and eat it that way. They made it look so delicious. I had some beans then took a big bite of my jalapeno pepper. Of course, I did not know what it was, but I found out in a hurry. I was chewing contentedly until it hit me again, that hot terrible burning in my mouth. I went through the burning torture all over again!

I could not understand how or why they put themselves through that torture. I could see that it did effect them although not as much as it did me. I could see a few of them breaking into sweats just like me but they did not stop eating the hot food. I guessed they were accustomed to the heat and discomfort.

The food was consumed at an alarming rate. It was disappearing almost as fast as it was being put on the table. When this had been going on for a while I saw many of the men start to push their plates away indicating they were through eating.

Without further words the leader stood and with a small nod to me, said, we would meet when Grandfather Sun arose and he left the hall. I was surprised he had not asked me anything. One of the elders told me before he left, the Grand Chief had to give some thought as to what he wanted to ask me. They would send for me in the morning. Everyone else walked toward the doors and left.

CHAPTER 5

PALOMITA

The servants had been taking the empty platters and bowls out as they were emptied. The room was almost clean as the last few people left the room. I looked around to ask someone what I should do, but before I knew it, I was alone in the big room. Even the tables had been cleared off. The only thing that had not been taken out was my drinking gourd which was still half full of water.

Left to myself I sat at the table thinking about everything that happened to me since I came to this new land. It was late and I was resigned to sleeping on the floor.

Then I heard a smaller side door open. The door was not hidden but very inconspicuous. I had not even noticed it. A very young girl of no more than sixteen summers, walked in the door. She was small, petite and had a narrow waist. Her hips flared out smoothly like any grown woman. I could tell that she was not a child because of the way her dress pushed out in front of her. Her breasts and nipples were very visible under her thin white dress. Her hair cascaded all the way to her waist and was so black it almost looked blue.

As I watched her moving around the room, I felt an old familiar stirring in my groin. I had been reared in a very spiritual way, but I was still a man in my prime. All her movements were pleasant to my eyes. I tried to look at her without staring. Everything about her was beautiful. It was her beauty, her body, and the way she went about doing things that captivated me.

The girl went from torch to torch extinguishing them in turn by throwing pieces of old hides on them. After she was done with that, she walked from one place to another picking up tanned hides and stacking them in one corner of the room. While doing her work, I could see her taking small side - glances at me. Her curiosity was getting the best of her.

In the corner, there were two low candleholders with large candles in them. There was also a small fireplace; I believed was for heating food than for warmth. It did create a comfortable atmosphere.

Before she smothered the last torch, she lit a candle. She put kindling and added more wood to the fireplace, and lit it. When she put out the final torch the place seemed dark vast hollow and quiet. With only one candle and the fire burning, the young girl had set a romantic mood.

The only sounds came from the small snapping and crackling of the fire and it gave me the feeling as though I was in a cave. It created a very mystical atmosphere. I still sat at the table wondering what was expected from me. I waited for her to leave but she did not. She knelt by the stack of hides. I thought it was to be my bed but she played with the hides until she had it right. She then produced a large white woven blanket and placed it over the hides. Finished with the bed she stood and turned to face me. Standing quietly, she acted as though she was afraid to talk to me or do anything first.

Was the girl to stay the night with me? Was she the last offering to the condemned man?

I finally talked to her. I asked her what she was waiting for. She told me that she was here to take care of me in all ways. Would I please come to the mats and lay down?

I told her she did not have to take care of me, as I was quite capable of looking after my own needs. I told her she did not have to stay and I did not want her to feel forced to do anything she did not want to. She explained that she had not been ordered to stay with me. She was asked if she wanted to and she said yes.

She walked to where I sat and said softly, "Come with me, Kokopelli," as she pulled me to my feet. I did not offer much of a protest nor hesitate getting to my feet.

She was young, beautiful, and alluring. I could smell some sort of spices on her breath. Her body smelled clean and with a scent of fresh flowers. I allowed her to pull me to the mats first. She made me sit, then lay back and relax.

I asked what her name was.

"Palomita," she answered. She said it meant Little Dove.

I could barely speak from feeling the emotion of passion rising within me but I managed to tell her it was a beautiful name and fit her perfectly.

This was not my first woman, but it had been awhile. I was tired, but I was too wound up from all that happened to notice it. I found out quickly that I was not as tired as I thought. When we are young, our bodies always seem to have the strength to bounce back and do whatever needs to be done. It was that way for me in my youth.

As I lay there, she removed my sandals. I felt her grab first one foot then the other and start massaging them with her fingers and thumbs. It was so quiet in the room I could hear her soft breathing.

I heard her splash some water from somewhere. Then with a piece of cloth she washed one, then the other foot. She washed me with small circular motions. The washcloth slowly traveled up my legs and my heart started pounding faster and harder. It traveled up one leg then the other. When I thought it was going to get interesting she stopped. I heard the water again and felt her start washing my face and neck. My eyes closed. I could smell the cloth and water she was using. It was clean and fresh. At her urging, I moved myself so I was laying full length on the mats. My robe had parted and as I shrugged my shoulders, it fell off and became part of the mat bed. I was completely naked.

Then it did get interesting. The wet washcloth and her little hands washed my private parts slowly and softly. That girl knew how to wash. It went on for just a few moments until she thought I was clean. Then she stopped.

I heard the faint whisper of cloth. Suddenly and quietly, she slipped on to the mat bed beside me. She was totally nude. This was unexpected and occurring so quickly, it took my breath away for a few seconds. I felt her hands moving all over me - feeling, touching, exploring. She was very sure of herself and knew how and where to touch. I was sure I was not her first man either.

I found myself responding to her. I returned her passion and kisses as passionately as she was giving them. I kissed her lips in desperation as though she might try to get away. She had built up a fierceness and tenderness in me I did not know I had. This foreplay went on until the candle burned to the thickness of one finger before I helped her climb up and straddle my waist.

My manhood was at the height of passion and very ready to explore and do what it was designed to do. I was not built very large but I was not small either. I was told that I was quite adequate.

She was so petite and small I was afraid I might hurt her but she would not let us stop. I lifted her with my hands encircling her waist and lowered her on to my manhood. She grunted, moaned, and let out her breath sharply but happily. She was now well impaled as she wiggled her small round bottom to get more comfortable. When she was settled, we moved slowly enjoying ourselves.

As the moments passed our emotions and our passions started to collide and erupt. We were experiencing the best sex a person can ever get and that is to have a simultaneous climax. We both erupted like volcanoes as convulsions rocked both our bodies. It went on for a few moments. Then both of us gasping and with our hearts pounding she rolled off to my side.

Spent, we held each other tenderly. We did not need to speak for a long while until her curiosity needed to be satisfied. She asked who I was, that she had heard my name was Kokopelli, but where had I come from? She said the word was going around that I had come from across the big water from where the sun rises every morning. How had I traveled to get here? If I did not walk or come in a boat then how did I arrive here?

The people are saying that you must be a God she said to me, they say you walk with Spirits but only Gods can do that. She wanted to know if I was a God. That was the reason she had been willing to sleep with me. It was a big honor to sleep with a God. She also said that everyone

31

loved my flute and the way I played it. People felt good when they heard it and it made them lose their anger. How had I learned to play it that way? All those questions she had for me and I could not answer them. She did not know I was asking the same questions of myself.

So they thought I was a God. I had never given a thought to my situation except I did not understand anything of what had happened to me nor why. Might I be a God and do not realize it? In my mind, I tried to use rationality to bring my brain into focus or balance. I certainly did not feel like a God. Then again, I did not know how a God should feel.

"No," I told Palomita, "I am not a God. I am a man just like any other man."

She looked at me sideways smiling and told me that as a God, I could not lie, but I could deny things to keep others from being hurt by their own thoughts.

No matter what I said, she would not believe me. She thought that I was only saying that to protect her in some way. Whatever I said would not matter to her; she wanted to be able to say to everyone that she had slept with the God that had come from where the sun rises each morning. She had slept with Kokopelli.

Now I understood why they had treated me the way they had, with respect and generosity. That was why they had not taken me prisoner and treated me as they had the others.

The union between Palomita and I had not been an act of love but a purely physical need which satisfied both of us. As lovers, we must treat each other with love and respect.

I kissed her and she jumped slightly as though afraid. She asked if I wanted her to leave. I replied that she could leave, but only if she wanted to. She wanted to stay with me all night if it was good with me. I asked what was wrong and she explained that most men, once done with a woman - threw them out, unless they were married to them. I told her that was not my way. Not long after we slept. When I woke the next morning Palomita was gone. I felt a pang of emptiness inside but only for a moment.

She left a long loincloth and a new clean robe folded on the floor next to the bed of mats. On top of them lay my flute and my sandals. After tying the loincloth and putting my robe over my left shoulder, I walked to the table. Where I had sat the night before there was both a cup of still steaming coffee, all ready to drink with goats' milk and honey in it. There was also a large clay cup filled with the sweet and warm chocolate. Palomita had given me a choice of what I might want to drink in the morning.

CHAPTER 6

GRAND CHIEF ATOLEH

The robe was the same as all elders wore. I chose to leave my right arm and shoulder uncovered, but only for the sake of being able to play my flute without hampering myself. I hoped it would not be too obvious and against tradition.

I sat at the table and sipped on my cup of hot coffee. I stood and sat down trying to get used to the loincloth. It felt strange but because of the material, it was comfortable. The clothing was made of a material from a plant instead of wool. They called it algodon (cotton) and it was made to fit loosely. The clothes kept the person cool from the humidity and heat.

My mind was running with different thoughts of what I had experienced so far. Meeting the Grand Chief and elders, stopping the execution of the prisoners, tasting the strange and wonderful food, were all mulling around in my head. Then I had my first romantic encounter in the new world, which was exquisite. The strangest thing of all I experienced so far was them thinking of me as a God. I was left to myself and had a chance to think things over.

These people eat well, I thought to myself. This is not like where I came from. There, it is difficult to raise crops and put food on the table. When life is this easy, it gives people the opportunity to study, experiment, and learn many good and useful things. It also gives them a chance to learn evil things and practice them if they choose to travel that path.

I asked myself what it was that I could offer or teach them. The one thing I saw, they may not have much of, was compassion and love for others. If they did not have compassion for others, then they would not have it for themselves. Compassion and love, I thought, is what I must help them learn to have for others and above all, themselves. The big question on my mind was what method or tool could I use to help them understand this new way of thinking. I prayed about it and asked that a way be shown to me.

Then I started to rethink my thoughts. Why had they not killed or at least taken me prisoner when I walked into the pyramid area? Everything seemed to start with the leaders and trickled down to the rest of the people. If they were cruel and unhappy then everyone below them was the same. On the other hand, if the leaders were intelligent and open to learning, then their ways would touch all their followers.

I remembered what Palomita had told me, that they thought I was a God. They treated me with respect because they thought I was a great being. Maybe they were afraid of me. I must treat them as equals because I did not want them to fear me. I did not want their respect in that way. One other thought crossed my mind. Perhaps they respected bravery, as did many other warrior societies. The way I walked into their village, some would believe me foolish. Yet others would think I was brave and courageous. They would honor me instead of kill me. I suppose I would never know what they thought, except I had been taken in and treated very well. Now I had to wait and find out which way the wind would be blowing on the new day.

I walked outside carrying the cup of café with my flute and my old robe tied across my back. My new clothes felt good though the loincloth still felt strange up under my manhood. I needed a little more room for my privates. I would have to pull the loincloth down occasionally until I became accustomed to it.

Standing in the patio of the big hall I finished my drink and set the cup next to the door. People walking by greeted me with a smile and a nod of respect. I wanted to yell and tell them that I was not a god and only a man. Then, if they believed me I might find myself in more trouble than I needed. I said nothing.

One of the Elders from last night came to me and after he greeted me asked if I could come and see Atoleh the Grand Chief of the Mayas.

Of course, I would go and see him; I was after all, his guest.

We found him seated in a small courtyard enclosure. It had high walls and several different fruit trees growing within it. There were pomegranate (granada) trees, peach (durasno), apricot (chavacan) and two very large fig (higo) trees. In one corner, there was a large fountain with the water cascading down several levels to the bottom. There were plants floating on the water and large orange fish swam lazily back and forth.

Sitting around the fountain were several girls and one elderly woman. I correctly thought she might be Atoleh's wife. As soon as the girls saw me, they started laughing and talking excitedly. They made very sure I noticed them until the older woman scolded them. They continued giggling and smiling at me.

It was difficult to talk and concentrate on my conversation with Atoleh. He told me that I had made quite an impression on Palomita, the girl who had spent the night with me. Many other rumors were going on about me, how I was the bringer of babies. Palomita swore she was going to have a child from me. Atoleh said she was a foolish girl and wondered how could she know so soon.

He invited me to join him as he dismissed the elder who brought me. I sensed he was uncomfortable. He did not know whether to be the Grand Chief and Ruler, or submit to the man he thought was a God. I thought I would put him at ease.

I thanked him for the company of Palomita the night before. Almost before I finished talking, he was waving me off, as though saying it was nothing. It may have been nothing to Atoleh but it certainly was something to me, and I am sure, Palomita.

Atoleh said, "Kokopelli, even a person such as yourself needs the company of a young woman occasionally."

I did not answer. I knew he was implying he felt I was someone special or godlike. I let him reach his own conclusions. I justified this by telling myself I had not lied to him. Now he wanted to know why I had come here. I thought to myself, if he thinks I am a God, and then I can let him believe it and say whatever I want with impunity.

Boldly, I explained, "I have found two things missing in your culture, in spite of your deep spirituality, your intelligence and powerful way of ruling your people."

He sat up straighter and asked what that could be. He thought he was being a good leader.

"You are one of the best leaders I have seen in my life," I answered. What I did not say was that he was in fact the only one I had ever spoken to that I could remember. "You are a good leader but you have allowed old traditions to distort what you want to do and accomplish." I was giving him credit for wanting and thinking of things, I was going to give and teach him.

"However, for you to continue to be a good ruler and leader you must stay open to new ideas and new ways of doing things especially for your people. Your kingdom and your country are your Spiritual Pyramid. You must always continue to climb it by seeking new knowledge and keeping an open and compassionate mind. For if you ever stop, it will mean that you have reached the top and the only way you can go then, is down. You will have lost your Spirit. Everyone has his or her own Spiritual Pyramid. They are climbing every chance they have to help someone. They climb each opportunity. They open their hearts to others with love and respect for everyone. Often the slope of the Pyramid gets very steep and hard to climb but if we persist, we get stronger and more capable. We must always attempt to keep climbing. If we do not reach the top it only means that we have not yet gained the wisdom and knowledge, we need to sit at God's side," I explained.

For a while, he sat as if he was in shock. It took a long thoughtful moment for him to think about what I told him. It was deep and contrary to his way of thinking, and difficult to absorb quickly. When he did come back from his thoughts he seemed desperate to find out what he was doing wrong. "Tell me, what am I doing wrong," he almost yelled at me, then looked at me apologetically and excused himself. He proclaimed, "I am willing to change things if they are for the better of the people."

Quietly I said, "Compassion is one of the goals we must search for in this life." I said it again. "Compassion, do you know what I mean by that?"

Atoleh admits the word is familiar but the meaning eludes him.

"Compassion, I tell him, is when you see a person that asks for forgiveness and you grant it to him. It means you have Compassion. Even if that person has done something you do not approve of and if he is a stranger. Compassion is the ability to forgive what he has done. It is also the ability to have pity on other people's feelings and pain. By setting that person free, you also set yourself free and your spirit grows. God will look at you differently, with respect, and will grant more of your prayers and wishes."

He looked at me with confusion on his face. It was such a strange concept; he was having trouble understanding it.

"God the Creator did not make all of us his children to just fight and kill each other for no reason. He wants us to grow and have large families, so there can be more of us to love and worship him. That is something else I want to show you. It is something called love. You must learn to love each other the way the Creator wanted. I have not seen any indication that you love and respect your women."

"Yes, we do love our women," he countered. "We let them cook and clean for us everyday and we take them to bed with us."

I shook my head slowly as though I could not believe what I was hearing.

Feeling that I was on safe ground, I put myself at his level. "Atoleh, my good friend, that is called lust not love. That is what I was guilty of last night. The Creator does not punish us for being human. He only chastises us if we intentionally hurt someone. It does not matter if we hurt them spiritually, emotionally, or physically - pain is pain. You must learn to respect and love your women. If you do this, you will see a big difference in the way they treat you in return. They will do so much more for you not only in the house but in bed also. They will bring you more sons to become warriors. Treat the women how you like to be treated yourself. Think of how they must feel when they are rejected. How would you take rejection? It is not easy to be abused and still smile."

Suddenly I see a strange look cross his face. It was as though he was waking up from a long sleep. I see realization dawning like the sun on his entire body.

"You mean like the Mexica warriors that are to be sacrificed tonight. If I give them their freedom, I will be showing compassion, and the Gods will look upon me with favor? Is this when my Pyramid is getting difficult to climb?" He asked.

"Yes, it is, but when you decide to change it then it will become easier. What do you believe the Creator will think? You are giving their lives back to them and they in turn will thank God for having saved them. Yes, he will know that you are a great and compassionate leader. Through your compassion, you will make them true believers of God.

"My enemies throughout the whole Land of Aztlan will think of me as weak and not fit to rule," He worried.

"To the contrary they will think of you as a strong ruler, Atoleh, for you keep your word, takes more courage than to kill those that offend you. They will know that you are not afraid to forgive and release men who have been your enemies."

"I must think and sleep on this, it is too much to think about all at once," He said with a sigh.

Then Atoleh stood up and motioned me to follow him. We moved only a few steps to a small table and chairs. As soon as we sat, two of the girls that had been doing all the chatter and giggling earlier started bringing out food for us. I found that it was about the same things we had to eat the night before including the frijoles (beans). I stayed away from the red sauce and meat. Now they brought something very good. It was a small thing tied up inside the leaves of the elote (corn). They called them tamales de elote. They were made from fresh ground corn, a long green chili pepper with cheese inside. It was very good and to my surprise only a little hot. It was not so hot that I could not eat it. After we had eaten our fill, we pushed back our chairs to relax. The leader of the Mayan people wanted some more answers so he asked more questions.

"Why do you think we do not treat our women right?" he wondered.

"It is not that you do not treat them right; it is that you do not show them enough respect. They work hard for you in all ways. All they have to look forward to is more things to do. Then when you are finished with them, you discard them. Be kind to them, treat them how you like to be treated yourself and you will find they will move mountains for you if you ask in the right way. Do not be afraid to be good to them. A strong leader fears nothing especially showing compassion and love in front of others. Most men who do not respect women and children act that way because they fear they are giving up control of something, when in reality they are losing the respect and love of those who mean the most to them," I offered.

"It seems that compassion and love are two things I can have in my life and still be comfortable with my place as a leader," realized Atoleh.

41

"By saying and thinking in just that way, you show you have grown into a giant of a man and leader, in God's eyes," I told him. I could see his pride and self-esteem grow around him.

"Then I do not have to think about it. I will start this day like a new man I will start showing compassion," he declared. "You may stay as long as you want for I could spend many suns like this talking and learning from you, but you must do as you must. I do not believe this is to be your only stop on your trail," he said.

"You are right, I have met you, a man of power, and I have done as the spirits told me. I have planted a seed. I ask only that you water it and when it grows, you in turn plant more seeds for the Creator and your people. You have nothing to do but gain from this," I said.

I could tell that he was happy with what he had learned that day. The rest of the day I saw runners come to his house, listening to him for a few moments then leave at a run. There were many changes coming to this part of the world.

CHAPTER 7

PLUMA ROSA AND FLORECITA

After Chief Atoleh left, I sat for a while and then went for a short walk around the garden. I spread a deer hide from my seat on the ground and dozed under the shade of one of the old fig trees. I was there until the sun was directly over me and one of the girls came to ask if I was hungry. I replied that I was getting that way but would like to bathe before eating.

"Good," she said and started giggling. She led me to a small bathhouse located behind all the trees, bushes and the garden. It was very secluded. As we walked, she turned and said, "They call me Florecita, it means Little Flower."

Once inside I saw a bathtub made of stone. The lighting was not bright like outside but it was light enough to see everything well. It reflected in from several small high openings. To one side was another small door. Another side of the opening was a round hole in the floor. It was for relieving yourself before going into the bathtub. I had asked the girl where to go by pointing to myself and acting as though I was urinating. She giggled and pointed to the smaller room. I went in and having to answer both calls, I squatted and answered nature's call. Nearby was a large clay pot with water and old eaten corncobs. It did not take me long to figure out how to use them. What I did not realize was that the overflowing water from the bathtub ran under the floor of the toilet and carried the waste away. Very ingenious, clean and accommodating

I was surprised to see water coming out of a stone pipe, which entered from under the wall. The water emptied into the tub keeping it constantly full.

I sat down on a low wooden stool to remove my sandals. The girl knelt down in front of me and pushed my hands away. She explained that she was there to take care of all the small things like this. She helped me undress then as I was getting into the water, she quickly disrobed too. She said with a smile she was to help me bathe and did not want to get her dress wet.

The girl was very forward and a bit aggressive but I did not mind at all. Although a little on the heavy side she was not fat. Her flesh was firm and she was muscular under the heaviness. She was young enough, about seventeen summers, that she could still have her child fat on her body. She was very pretty and had white, even teeth and a beautiful smile. She moved with determination and without wasting any energy or motion. She was in the bath and splashing water on my back.

I heard a rustle of cloth behind me. Turning to look I was surprised to find the other girl that had also served me food taking off her clothes. The new girl said, "Let me help you bathe him, he is too big for you all alone."

Laughing, Florecita told Pluma Rosa (Pink Feather) she was right to step into the tub and help her do the job well. Pluma Rosa had a nice slender body. She could have passed as Palomita's sister except she was not as pretty!

Pluma Rosa was even more aggressive than her companion was; she went directly to my manhood and gave a cry of joy when she found it hard, proud, and ready.

Reluctantly she released it to do what they were there to do, give me a bath.

Happily, they each took one of my arms and with a scrubber (loufa pad) started washing me. They used something that quickly foamed up. I asked what it was, as they put some on my head and beard to wash. They said it was the sweet saliva of the yucca plant; it washes us very well and takes off all the sweat and dirt. They each pulled one of my feet up and I had to sit on the edge of the large bathtub. They washed my feet and massaged them until they started to tingle. Then they playfully pulled me back into the water.

When there are two women washing you, there is only one result - an erection that needs to be taken care of.

Pluma Rosa being the more aggressive of the two found it again as she washed me lower and lower. She let out a small cry of happiness and exclaimed that she was done with the washing part. She moved and positioned herself in front of me leaning forward to kiss me warmly. Quickly she grabbed me, found her center, and threw her legs around me to take full advantage of what she had found under the soapy, slippery water. Of course, I had to help and hold her up in the water while she got all the movements done. She must have been thinking very hard about this because it was not long before she threw her head back and let out several loud hissing breaths.

While she was enjoying herself, Florecita was hugging my head, kissing my ear and playing with herself under the water. The water suddenly felt much warmer.

As Pluma Rosa's legs slipped off my waist, Florecita said it was her turn, and moved around in front, as she slipped my manhood into her opening. It felt hot and tight but good, very good.

Like I said before my penis was not big, but it is not very small either. I was finding out that the women here were built small but only between the legs. That made my size a very nice tight fit. That made it feel better for everyone concerned.

Florecita must have done wonders with her fingers because within a very few moments after she had straddled me, she was moaning and jerking about fiercely as she hung on to me with her arms around my neck. I had to hang on to her buttocks, holding one in each hand as I moved in and out of her. Her movements, jerking, and moaning were having their effect on me. I was also quickly getting ready to reach the top. I tried to prolong it as long as I could but we were both too far over the top to hold back. We both went into convulsions together and finished together.

It was not over. Pluma Rosa gently pushed Florecita away and said that she also wanted to have a baby from me. She reached out under the soapy water searching and finding my still hard manhood. She laughed happily and asked if I could go again. I told her that it was up to her if she could get me there; I was willing to try.

She mounted herself again on my erection and I started helping her moving her up and down. Florecita would not to be left out. She joined us again and helped me get excited by kissing and massaging me all over. Her hands went under the water to play and touch me. I had not gone over the hill inside Pluma Rosa and that was what she wanted. We quickly reached the very special place and went over the top together.

After we were done with our pleasures, we relaxed in the water. The two girls washed me all over again. I stepped up out of the tub and they playfully moved around me drying me off.

They looked at me smiling, then at each other, when they saw my manhood start rearing its head again. "No, that was enough for now," I said as I stood up to dress.

Quickly they dressed throwing on their robe style dresses. Smiling, they left saying they would have the food ready for me when I was ready to eat. It crossed my mind that Chief Atoleh had already told them they were going to have more rights now and more respect. I loved the results. The bath turned into a very exciting hour of pure delight. I was twice as hungry as I was before the bath started.

I went back to the small table and sat down to eat. They brought all different kinds of food. They did bring some hot food and they encouraged me to eat. They said it would make my blood hot too. Florecita laughed and made a comment that I did not need it. They also brought steamed oysters and clams. They had a platter with a large baked whole fish.

They told me that the Big Waters were not too far, to where the Sun rises each morning. That is where the fish and ocean food came from fresh every morning. The fish had slept in the ocean the night before, as had the clams. They encouraged me to eat more clams than anything else did, because they said it put strength back into my manhood. After this morning, I would need to get my strength back.

One of the other girls walked to the table smiling at me with a mischievous look on her face and placed a large basket of fruit on the table. There was one they called mango, platano (banana) and one called papaya to name a few. Pluma Rosa sliced a few of them for me. I tried at least a bite of each one of them. All were different but I liked all of them.

I think that the gossip about the two girls and I in the bathhouse was already making the rounds before we were out of it. The two girls trying to out do each other were making me out to be bigger than I could ever be. I learned to let them think what they wished; they would make things larger than life all by themselves.

That afternoon I ate until I could eat no more. It had been the biggest feast I ever had my entire life or since I could remember. Food was indeed bountiful here.

I spent the evening alone with two girls waiting on me as though I was the Grand Chief himself. I thought I could get used to this but knew that was impossible and not to be. It was not my path. After eating, the small room attached to the bathhouse, was ready for me to sleep in. The skins were piled in the corner and the candles were lit. That night was also very interesting. I had two companions all night trying their best to please me. They made me feel very special. It was difficult for me but what could I say or do? I had an image to keep up. They made me feel very special indeed.

The next morning I was called to break fast with Chief Atoleh. Apparently, he had heard about the girls' visit to my room the night before and was smiling at me.

"You are staying very busy I hear, Kokopelli," He commented.

I just nodded my head hoping I was not offending anyone. I just waited to see what he had to say next. The

48

Chief said he did not remember if he extended an invitation to me to remain as long as I wanted to. If he had not I was welcome to use the sleeping room by the bathhouse for as long as I was there. I thanked him for his generosity and told him I did not know how long I would remain but accepted his invitation. He waved away my words as though I did not need to say anything. He also said to have the girls, anyone of them, to do whatever I needed done and they were at my disposal. I was to feel free to look and walk around as much as I wanted.

They would be happy to have me as their permanent guest if I chose to remain. He told me he was going to be busy for a few suns and must go to other outlying villages such as Cobasa, Edzntna, Uxmal and Mayapan to name a few. He said he went there to settle arguments and disputes. One of his trusted military leaders collected his taxes. He had to do this twice within the seasons, once in the spring and once in the fall.

CHAPTER 8

MEDIA LUNA

A sun later after he left to do his Chieftain duties I received a call from the High Priest Media Luna to come and see him at the pyramid as soon as I was able. He heard that I was very busy.

I sent word with the same runner I would be there shortly, as soon as I finished breaking my fast. I was indeed happy and thankful to have something different to do, though I loved it, the thought of just lying around another day did not sit well with me. I was starting to get restless. Resting and enjoying the fruits of the land was beginning to be to commonplace. That is not good for the body, mind, or the Spirit.

I left shortly after the runner. It was not a far distance, and with my long strides, I almost arrived before the runner. As I strode through the crowds of people, they would greet me with smiles and nodding heads. I also nodded and smiled in return. They seemed to be a happy and kind people.

They made me feel very welcome, happy and almost like home. I could hear my name whispered as the people stepped aside for me. "Kokopelli, Kokopelli," I heard. I was happy they knew who I was.

The High Priest Media Luna seemed to be waiting for me. He greeted me with a smile and a firm arm grip. As a greeting, these men gripped their right forearms just above the wrist. I analyzed the reason and concluded that when they greeted each other this way, each man knew the other was not holding any weapons. It showed they could be trusted.

His actions were friendly and he seemed to want to talk with me but I could still feel some underlying reservations. He had a nervous way about him although he hid it well. It was more of a feeling I got from him than anything I could actually see was.

This Elder I knew had been around many seasons for he was old, stooped and his long hair that cascaded to his waist, had all turned gray. A person could see the wisdom in his eyes and the pain in his movements. Though thin and old, he was still strong. He still seemed to have all his teeth for when he smiled they were visible. He apparently had good vision; his eyes were sharp and clear. His back was beginning to bow and pull him down. He must be in pain from stiffening joints.

From the back of my mind I remembered someone telling me that drinking salt minerals diluted in water in moderation, would help dissolve the accumulation of calcium in the joints. That would help stop the pain. When he was ready to listen, I would tell him about it.

He surprised me by asking a question without hesitation, "Why are you here? Where did you come from?"

Before I could answer the first questions he asked, "How I had reached the settlement without being spotted by the guards?"

Before I answered him, I looked at him for several long moments. I knew only the truth would be right. If I tried to deny anything, he would see it, and know I was not to be trusted. This would be a betrayal, and he would forever be my enemy.

"To answer your first question, I came here to gain some of your wisdom and knowledge."

"Why do you want to learn what I know and what would you do with what you learn?" He asked.

"I want to take your wisdom to other people and make them wiser and more tolerant of others and themselves."

"As for your second question, as I told Atoleh, I cannot find in my memory how I got here. I sincerely wish I knew the answer to that question. I have asked it of myself many suns. I do not know how I traveled here. One moment I was not and the next instant I found myself walking through the dense and humid brush following a very distinct trail. The only answer I have is the Creator wishes for me to spread the seeds of knowledge that I carry with me, not only here, but also throughout other lands. To spread the seeds brought to me as far and for as long as I am able to travel."

He looked at me long and hard. Then he asked me if I thought I was or claimed to be a God.

I replied quickly, "No I was not a God and had never claimed to be one." Perhaps I replied too quickly as though I had practiced my answer.

With a look of satisfaction, he said that is the answer he thought I would give. He was in fact thinking as the girls had thought, that I was denying it only because it was indeed the truth. Here I thought that as a Spiritual man he would know the truth when he heard it. Never did I dream that he would not believe me. I sincerely thought he would believe what I told him and he could help me find the reason I was here and what I was supposed to be doing. He believed only what he wanted to believe.

While he was thinking and assessing what I had told him, I glanced up toward the top of the pyramid. I was so close to the base I could not see the top. It seemed to disappear into it. I stepped away to see better and I still could not see the top. It seemed to go upward forever. The steps went upward into the heavens or so it seemed.

With a small bow of respect, he invited me to ascend the pyramid with him. We started climbing. We went up, up, and still further up. I had not realized how high this place of worship was. He explained to me as we climbed, "The ceremonies are held here as high as possible and as close to the Gods as can be humanly done. But, Kokopelli, I am sure you already knew this."

Half way to the top we stopped at a place where many people could stand while ceremonies were taking place at the same level or at the top of the pyramid. This was when he talked about things and his feelings about me.

As we stood catching our breath I turned and looked around at what I thought was a big village. I was quite astounded to see how truly vast it was. It was in fact a very large city and it stretched for many leagues in the three directions. I could see several more pyramids of different sizes. I was impressed. I had never seen, much less imagined a settlement could be so far reaching.

He told me he had predicted and always told the people that one day Father Sun would send lesser Gods, but Gods never the less, to study them and see if they were doing their duties in the right way. He knew I had been sent, and that I could not tell anyone who I truly was. If I did, everyone would be on their best behavior. Ever since Media Luna had been the High Priest, he knew my being here proved he had been correct in his prediction.

The things he wanted to ask me had been few, though they had been important to him. He had found out what he wanted to know. He was satisfied with what he had learned from me.

We sat down looking at the city and masses of people as they walked from place to place. From a pocket in his robe, Media Luna brought out a small clay pipe and a pouch of what I thought was an herb. He told me whenever he truly wanted to be alone or to help his spirit fly he would smoke a special herb that was brought to him for just that purpose. Media Luna told me the Medicine People had used this herb for eons. It gave them the ability to see their visions more clearly.

He filled the small pipe and from one of the burning urns he got a hot coal and put it in his pipe. He drew on it inhaling while drawing in air with the smoke. He choked a little but with shear determination held the smoke in. He offered me the pipe and nodded for me to draw on it. He had shown me how it was done and I was a quick learner.

Putting the pipe to my lips, I drew on it and did not do it as he had. I took in a big mouth full then tried to breathe inward. When the harsh smoke hit the back of my throat I choked, as I never had before. I started coughing and choking. I coughed, coughed, and could not stop. A good amount of smoke never the less got through to my lungs. It was not very long before the coughing subsided and my head started spinning. I felt like I was floating, that my feet were off the pyramid. I felt light and alive but very strange.

My face lost all feeling. I touched it and it had a dead feeling to it. I had to sit before I fell. Media Luna was looking at me with a smile on his face. Suddenly I was back on my feet and he was offering me the pipe again. I could not remember when he had taken it back. I asked him what in the world had he put in the pipe.

He explained it was called marijuana. It was a special herb that had been given to the Medicine People to be used in prayer and ceremony. They had been gifted another herb that came to them from the desert country many suns to the north. It was called peyote and grew only in the desert.

I asked if it was used the same as this and if it was as strong.

"No," He replied, "That one you have to chew and swallow the saliva in order for it to work for you. You ask if it is as strong. It is stronger than this, but is also very spiritual. I will let you have some of it at the next ceremony."

I said reluctantly, "If it was that strong I would rather leave it for other people to use."

He said, "You should at least try it, but if you do not want to, that is good also. For every person should know his or her direction and goals."

"Yes," I said, "My decisions are my destiny and I must make them with great care."

It had been a different and strange experience, but not something I wanted in my life. I felt that if a person smoked the herb or chewed peyote for guidance and visions he was not in his right mind and may misinterpret what he saw and get in trouble with the spirits.

Media Luna finished smoking the pipe. I sat down to enjoy the quiet as the sun was dipping below the horizon. I do not know what Media Luna was doing except that he was now happy and talkative.

For the remainder of our stay on top of the Great Pyramid he proudly pointed out other important sites within our vision. He was very proud of what his people had accomplished, as it should be. They were far more advanced than any other people I knew of were.

I was surprised how quickly our visit had passed being so close to the heavens. Before I realized it, the sun was almost ready to set in the western horizon. We descended the pyramid in silence. He was preoccupied with trying to figure me out still not knowing if I was who he thought I was or someone else. I on the other hand was still thinking of what I had seen. I was very impressed and now questioned myself even more. What can I offer or teach a people such as these who are so intelligent and advanced?

When we got to the bottom of the pyramid, we faced each other so I could thank him for the knowledge he had given me. Before I could say anything, he asked me if I had liked the feeling I had from the marijuana we had smoked. Once again, I said no, it had not been a very pleasant or spiritual experience for me.

He said, then he would not offer it to me again, but if I ever needed or wanted it to ask him. He gave me a strong-arm shake, a half hug and bid me a good night. He left quickly becoming lost in the dark and drifting haze.

CHAPTER 9

MY FIRST TEMASCAL

I returned to my little sleeping house as darkness fell. I found a small table with food set out on it covered with a clean piece of white cloth. There were also small candles lighting the area good enough so I could see. Close by a large seashell had some kind of leaves smoldering in it. There was mosquitoes flying around and it was keeping them away. I ate alone for a change and very sparingly. It was not good to lay down with a very heavy stomach. I missed the girls, but they must have thought I needed rest. They did not return until the following morning.

A few suns rose and set. The season was moving ever so slowly. I bathed with one girl and on occasion two of them, but it seemed that I never bathed alone. It was good because seldom did I bathe with the same girl twice in succession. Sleeping arrangements were the same thing, always at least one, some evenings, two.

These women were not loose girls. They were just healthy, excited young girls with their hormones going wild and looking for someone to help them release their pent up energy. I was fortunate to be picked by them and be there for them when it happened. They talked among themselves, but they did not run around yelling it to the world. They were very discreet about it. In fact, they always left my sleeping quarters well before Grandfather Sun saw them as he rose above the jungle treetops.

One morning after the Chief returned he sent one of the girls to call me. It was earlier than usual so I thought there must be something important about to occur. I was right. As soon as I got to the table, he motioned me to sit and eat. As I was served my plate of food, he told me that evening they were having a very important ceremony, and would I like to take part in it?

Not having had an opportunity to do much except taste and savor the local fruits, I was anxious to see another part of these people's culture. I wanted to learn and see some of their ways. It was important for me to learn, perhaps this way I could see if I was indeed needed to help them. I enthusiastically agreed to attend.

He told me to relax until midday, then he would send for me and we would leave. Prepare yourself mentally he said, and that I would need a lot of strength and courage. That it was a very hard and demanding ceremony.

I followed his advice. After breaking fast, I went back to my quarters and did a few exercises. I pulled the bow from both sides and scraped the hide a few repetitions. I rowed the canoe until I began to tire then stopped to rest and relax. These exercises I developed to keep fit when I was unable to walk, run, or do other things. I actually developed twelve but I believed these were the most important to me now.

One of the girls came into my room quietly and asked if she could be of any service to me. I replied that I was in meditation and needed to rest. She asked if I was going to take part in the ceremony. I answered that I was. She told me that she would not let anyone disturb me that I had to rest. She slipped out as quietly as she had come in.

That started me thinking. What was this ceremony that was going to be so hard on me that I needed to rest before I went? I had no idea so all I could do was wait and see.

It was not long when another of the girls came to tell me the Grand Chief was ready to go. I walked out of my little room and wondered if I was ever going to see it again. Meeting the Grand Chief in front of the house, followed by his hand servants we walked off without a word.

We walked beyond the pyramid. We walked on around it for quite a distance and finally stopped where a large group of men was standing around a fire. Most of them had the robes around their shoulders. I thought that they must be priests. Standing close but a little apart from them was the High Priest Media Luna. As The Grand Chief and I arrived, he came to where we stopped. The others all respectfully moved aside giving us room and privacy.

Media Luna was surprised to see the Grand Chief present at the ceremony. He immediately asked the Grand Chief if something was wrong or if there was something he could do for us. The Grand Chief replied he had never thought about taking part in the ceremony before. He now felt he should find out about it and why it was part of the priests learning. He noticed they were always willing to take part in the ceremony. He also told the High Priest that both of us were here to learn and would be his students. He was to run the ceremony as he always did as though we were not present.

With a relieved look on his face Media Luna said he would be honored to teach them the little he knew.

He started moving slowly and asked if we would follow him. We got in the shade of an old cottonwood tree and stopped. Two of the younger men hurriedly spread out a small hand woven rug for each of us to sit. After we were comfortable, he began to talk quietly.

He explained he had a vision through a powerful dream. The Spirits had shown him how to build the small sweathouse lodge out of the baked bricks. The Spirits gave him some information, but told him he had to see what else he needed and to find ways of conducting the ceremony.

Things had to come to him from his heart so it would have more meaning to everyone involved. They did not leave him alone; the Spirits would bring him dreams almost on a nightly basis. Small pieces of information came to him that he understood and wove into the ceremony as he was doing today. The way of doing this ceremony had taken him several summers and winters to put together.

The High Priest explained that he called it a Temascal (Sweat Lodge). He did not explain why. The reason we had the ceremony was to sweat out all the impurities from our bodies while purifying our spirits. This was done through sacrificing our bodies to very intense heat. After we were pure of body, mind, and spirit, we could feel comfortable asking the Creator to listen to our prayers. It purged our bodies of bad medicine and negative energies that could be attached to us. The heat was brought into the lodge through the red hot Grandfather rocks.

He told us that for many moons he had been teaching some of the local younger men that were not yet priests, how to help him with the fire. He would teach them the songs so they might know and pass them on to others.

He went on to explain that the Medicine people and priests would purify first then the fire keepers, who were young men that wanted to follow the Spiritual path. Then the others would take their turn in the lodge. Always they would fit in as many as possible to give everyone the opportunity to participate. In the Temascal, no one was better than anyone else was. In the dark we are all God's children and all equal. The only reason the priests had their ceremony first is because they must return to their places of worship and attend to the sick and pray for the weak.

Media Luna explained further about the reason we would do certain things and how we would do them. "First," he said, "When we go into the Temascal we crawl in on our hands and knees. In that way, we show the Great Spirit and Creator that we are willing to humble ourselves to him for his blessings and answering our prayers."

When entering, we would stop at the door and say the words, "Oma Teo." It is hard to translate, but it was brought to us to thank the Creator for all there is and for all duality: the good, the bad; the day, the night; the female and male. In others words the Balance to all life and all that exists.

The Grand Chief in awe repeated the word in a whisper, "Oma Teo." He said it was a powerful word. It must be treated and said only in a respectful way.

The High Priest felt he had given us enough to think about for now. He left us to direct all the other things going on. He went to some men that had a drum and asked them to start drumming and singing. He told them to sing the appropriate songs for loading (filling) the pipe and whatever the ceremony called for. After he had instructed some men about the fire, he called to show us what he was going to do next.

The High Priest called us to where he was sitting on the ground. He told us we would now fill the Sacred Pipe to

61

honor the Gods and Spirits of the Seven Sacred Directions and wanted us to see how it was done.

In front of him, he had a small deerskin pouch where he had his own tobacco mixture. Out of a long buckskin bag, he brought out first, a long pipe stem, then a beautifully carved black stone pipe. He purified his Sacred Pipe over an abalone shell that had hot coals and Copal smoldering in it. He took a small pinch of tobacco and honored the Spirits of the east direction first. Then he repeated the motion to the south direction, saying a prayer quietly in each direction. He continued until he had honored Father Sky, Mother Earth, and the Spirit Within our bodies.

After he was finished with the pipe he laid it down on a small mound of dirt that was located just in front of the Temascal's opening.

Getting up he turned to me and said if I wanted to take some of his knowledge and wisdom with me to take this ceremony of the Temascal (Sweat Lodge) to other people and other lands. This ceremony would benefit and help everyone who chose to take part in it. It belongs to anyone who respected and used it in a good way. This, he said is the most powerful Medicine of all. Oma Teo! He repeated as though wanting the power of that word to embrace me and me to embrace it. I did with all my heart.

The fire I noticed was built in a slight depression. There was a small square, low, red brick building not far from the fire pit. It was as high as my chest and quite small. It was only about five paces from the fire. There were small openings about half way up the walls covered with deer hides. Above the small door was a large hide that looked like it might be from an ox. Right next to the opening, there were three clay pots full of water and one large gourd with a dipper gourd inside. I had no idea how they were used. I thought they might be for drinking in the lodge during the ceremony. I would find out soon enough.

The opening faced the fire. I wondered what kind of ceremony used such a large fire. I found out shortly after the High Priest had finished loading his Sacred Pipe.

He called for all of us to get ready. The Grand Chief stood looking and waiting to see what everyone else was going to do. The lower Priests dropped their robes wearing only their loincloths. Some of them took the loincloths off to go in to the lodge completely naked. Others tied their loincloths around their waists.

I took my robe off then turned and spread it out in front of the Grand Chief to give him some privacy when he decided which way he was going to enter the lodge. He decided to wear only his loincloth, but the High Priest quietly advised him to also carry his robe in under his arm.

I thought I would do the same and carry my robe into the lodge not knowing what I was getting into. I removed my loincloth and tied it around my waist. I believed it might be more comfortable.

We all gathered and lined up close to the small entrance to the lodge.

Another of the younger priests walked to the front of the lodge and raised a large seashell called a conch shell to his lips. Facing to the East, he blew on it. The sound was loud, beautiful, and haunting. It made my skin feel like it was crawling. He continued to blow the conch shell to other Sacred Directions. As he turned to blow it in a different direction, we all turned and faced the same way. It was done with such intensity, that in it self was a ceremony.

When he was done, the High Priest instructed the priest who had blown the shell to cleanse (smudge) each of us before crawling into the lodge. The one doing the smudging was using a large blue wing fan from a bird like the one I had taken the fruit.

After being smudged, the High Priest went in first. Then he dropped to his knees and crawled into the lodge. "Oma Teo!" He said loudly. He was teaching us by setting an example.

One by one, we were smudged and followed his lead. It was very strange to me, the crackling hot fire, the smell of wood smoke, the strong smell of Copal burning, and some of the men drumming and singing in the background.

When the Grand Chief went in, I was right behind him. We crawled until we got to where the others were sitting and put our backs against the wall. We ended up very close to the opening. All we could do was wait to see what was going to happen next. It was very dim inside and already hot, though it did not bother me. I did not know yet what was coming.

When the last man was in the Temascal, the High Priest asked for his Sacred Pipe to be handed to him. The fire keepers also handed him a small hand drum and a pair of large deer antlers. The Grand Chief and I sat there quietly taking in all these things that were being brought in and wondering how they were all used.

The High Priest spoke a few words of encouragement. He explained a little to those of us that had never experienced this before. He could not or would not tell us anymore. We were grown men and were up to the challenge.

He called to the fire keepers to bring in twenty stones. He also asked one of the other men if he would bless the grandfathers as they were brought in. He handed the man a pouch that had dry, ground up, Copal. He was to sprinkle a small amount on to each stone as it came in.

The fire keeper using a thick, green tree branch pulled the red-hot stones out of the high mound of hot coals. The other fire keeper grabbed the first one with a large Elk antler and brought it into the lodge. He put it on the floor and the young man next to the door moved it to the center of the hole in the center of the Temascal with the two deer antlers. Now I knew why the antlers were in the lodge.

"Oma Teo!" Said Media Luna the lodge leader, greeting the grandfather stone as he touched it with the Sacred Pipe. The man with the copal sprinkled it on. The beautiful smell of the tree sap permeated the small enclosure.

"Oma Teo," I said.

Media Luna looked up sharply, not liking the interruption. Realizing who had spoken, he asked quietly what I wanted. I asked if I could help place the stones in the center.

He replied that if I still wanted to help after the first round, he would let me, but first, I must look and learn only. I sat back quietly. I already had a deep feeling in my heart that this was some of the knowledge I was seeking. It was going to be something I would love and cherish.

Immediately the temperature went higher in the lodge. The fire keepers kept repeating their movements bringing in stone after hot stone.

"Oma Teo," Media Luna greeted each stone with his beautiful black Pipe.

The man putting the Copal on the stones got a little heavy handed with it. The air was so heavy with the Copal smoke it was getting hard to breathe and harder still to see the others on the other side of the lodge.

Inside, the Temascal kept getting hotter and hotter, until there were twenty hot stones in the center. Some of the first ones brought in were turning a dark gray color. They were losing their heat and I could feel where the heat was going.

The High Priest handed out his Sacred Pipe and asked for the water and his drum. The large gourd now half full of water was passed in. The small dipper gourd was floating on the water. The man by the door helped the Head Priest touch the large gourd to the stones asking for a blessing on the water.

Finally, Media Luna asked the door to be closed. One of the fire keepers outside pulled the large hide down over the entrance. The Temascal was plunged into total darkness. The only thing I could see was a red glow from the stones in the center.

Slowly, I started hearing the drum, then the sound increased ever so slightly. The High Priest started singing a very beautiful song. He was honoring and asking for a blessing for the people of Chi-Chen Itza. He sang with such a beautiful voice, I was having trouble believing it was the High Priest singing. There was no other sound in the lodge except his voice. I almost stopped breathing, and it seemed everyone else did. I listened, his words touched my heart, and I knew why he was High Priest of the Mayan people.

When he finished singing, I heard him rattle the small gourd in the large water gourd. I heard the water splash then it hit the hot stones. He poured one, two, three, then more and more water on the stones. I thought I knew what hot was until he did that.

It got so hot in the lodge I thought I was being cooked alive. I started praying hard for guidance and the courage to survive this new ceremony. I had not known what to expect and I found it very difficult to concentrate on my prayers. I put my chin on my chest and thought of that thin, frail man running the ceremony. If he can stand this, so can I. My thoughts were, I would last through the whole ceremony.

He stopped pouring water for the moment and started praying. He prayed long and hard for the many things he knew were needed in his country. He asked the Creator for help in teaching the ones that wanted to learn. The praying went on for quite a long while.

The heat had no where to go so it remained there around us and stayed as hot as it had been when he poured the water. Slowly, slowly the temperature seemed to lessen just long enough for us to catch our breath, and then he poured more water on hot stones. It did not take the lodge long to start baking us again.

By now, I was ready. I stilled myself and prayed as hard as I could. The biggest thing I asked for was to be shown the reason I was here and what I was supposed to do. It did not seem to be as long and I heard him empty the rest of the water in the gourd.

"Oma Teo," he yelled loudly. He was letting the fire keepers know he wanted the door opened.

Cool, clean air rushed into the small lodge. I felt as though we had received a gift of air to bring new life to us. I relaxed thinking the ceremony was finished. Then the High Priest asked me if I wanted to welcome the Grandfather stones with the Copal this round. I said I was ready to learn if he would show me how.

He handed the pouch of Copal and told me to sprinkle a small amount on each stone as it was placed in the center. I silently said a prayer that I would not make any mistakes.

Once again, the High Priest asked for twenty more stones to be brought in. It felt good to be the one greeting the Grandfathers as they were brought into the lodge.

Though different, I knew what to expect and learned on the first round how to focus and direct my energy. It was very hot again; the hot steam from the stones had nowhere to go. It stayed right on us while the door was closed. It was a wonderful opportunity to pray and seek direction.

The door opened and was left open for quite a while. The High Priest allowed us to talk and visit as we recuperated. Again, he called out to the fire keepers to bring in the rest of the stones. He wanted any stones the size of a fist or larger if any had broken. If my counting was correct, they would be bringing in forty or more stones.

I hope I can handle that many stones I thought to myself. Then I turned and looked at the Grand Chief. I had not heard a single noise out of him. He looked relaxed and happy to be in there. He was taking the ceremony very well. I saw Media Luna looking at us and I think it surprised him we were both doing well.

Two of the others had asked to be let out and they were allowed to leave. I noticed when the door was open; several of the men were laying down. I was surprised because I had not thought of doing that. It must not be against the rules to do that for our leader had said nothing.

They started bringing in the stones and I put the Copal on as I welcomed them. When the stones were finally all in, they formed quite a large pile in the center of the lodge.

It did not take long to get hot again. I had trouble breathing. The steam burned the inside of my nostrils and if I tried to breathe through my mouth it burned also. My eyelids felt as though they would blister, but they did not. It must have felt hot to Media Luna. He knew it was very hot for us. Showing us what a good leader always does, he had compassion and opened the door not long after this.

The cover was off the door a few moments, and then he had it closed again. He said a wonderful prayer that included the Grand Chief, his family, and me. I was grateful when he yelled to have the door opened again.

We crawled out, each of us saying the sacred words, "Oma Teo," as we left the lodge. The ceremony was over.

Once out we stood and dried ourselves off and talked quietly. I noticed two large tables were set up and covered with food. Most of what I could see was fruits of all kinds. Media Luna called for everyone to eat. He directed Chief Atoleh and I toward a large tree where there were three chairs under its shade. After we sat down, two of the young men brought us a small table laden with food and fruit.

We spent another good part of the late afternoon eating, drinking, and sharing our first experience in the Temascal. Media Luna asked what we thought of the Temascal. Chief Atoleh said he now understood more about what attracted men to this ceremony. He told Media Luna he felt cleaner and uplifted, more than he ever felt in his life, both physically and spiritually.

I told him I was glad this way was shown to me, as it was part of the knowledge I was seeking. I asked permission to carry this knowledge with me and show others this powerful way to pray. Media Luna explained that my learning was not over. He said I needed to do this ceremony at every opportunity, so that I could pass it on to others. He further explained that when you are leading a ceremony such as this, you are asking the Spirits to come in and listen to your prayers. The leader has to learn how to call in the good spirits and keep the bad or negative spirits away. This is an important part of the Temascal and is only learned from experiencing many ceremonies.

Chief Atoleh and I walked slowly followed by his hand servants, back to his residence and my little corner hut. We were both tired and spent. The sun was low in the western horizon. As we walked, shoulders almost touching, he asked me quietly if I had any other thoughts about the Temascal.

I told him after thinking about it for a moment, that this was a good way for people to offer themselves as a sacrifice to get prayers answered, without anyone having to shed blood. It was a way to get the Creator's attention, and an opportunity to spread the word about love and compassion. "Yes, Chief Atoleh, I liked this beautiful ceremony and I will carry it to other people wherever I go." I humbly answered him.

I had not asked Media Luna if women could do this. I could not see why they should not be able to. They are also the Creator's children and life givers. Women also pray and I am sure they ask the Creator to answer their prayers.

I smiled to myself at my boldness. Here I was, completing only one Temascal or Sweat Lodge ceremony and I was already making decisions and questioning who could do the ceremony. I had to learn quickly and spread the knowledge widely. I felt that life, as we knew it was fast coming to an end. Things would be changing rapidly in the near future and the people would need this Spirituality to help them endure the changes.

There would be many different religions and alien beliefs shown to the people. It would cause confusion and distrust among the natives. Though I was not a born native of this country, I felt they were my relatives because of the mission the Creator had given me. I felt very close to them. How could I see them as different from me, for are we not all God's children and therefore all related?

I continued to talk as we walked. "Can you see how it is better to suffer and sacrifice yourself than to take the life of another? When all mankind begins to think this way, the Creator will know that he has done his work right, by teaching us these ways. He will know that we have learned justice, humility, and compassion. These are the three most important things a person must learn to have a full and bountiful life."

When I finished talking, we were stepping into the courtyard of the Grand Chief's home. We stopped and without words gripped each other's right arm in a warm arm shake and a one arm embrace and wished each other a good night.

I had given him much to think over. I had to look deep within myself and think of all that happened, as it had been a long day. I was tired and not hungry at all. I went straight to the small room and relieved myself into the round hole in the floor. Finding my bed I slipped off my robe, pulled off my sandals, and rolled on to my back. I was sound asleep as the crickets and night frogs serenaded each other in the night.

The next morning, I had broken my fast and was sitting enjoying the morning. A young man, who was at the Temascal, walked up and told me he had been sent by Media Luna to be at my service and help with anything I needed.

I asked him his name. In almost the same breath I told him, that everything I would need was being taken care of by the young women from the house.

He replied that his name was Tuleco. He said there were many things he could do for me that the women could not. He was there to help, carry and do things for me. He said that he was young and strong. The most important reason he wanted to be my manservant, was he wanted to learn all I would teach him.

The path he had chosen was the Spiritual path and there was no better place to learn, than with someone who walks with spirits. He also told me that every one of the young men who helped Media Luna had wanted to come. They had to draw stones that were all black except one it was white and he had drawn it. That is why he had come. He felt the Gods had been smiling at him.

For many suns after that first Temascal, almost every sun, Tuleco would come and ask if I wanted to purify and learn. I never said no. I learned much and experienced more. Then after sweating and purifying for many suns Media Luna called me to talk. He asked how I felt about this ceremony now. I replied that I loved it and he should know I had not missed one ceremony for many suns. He asked if I thought I was ready to help others with these ways. I answered him with a question of my own by asking if he thought I was ready. Without hesitating, Media Luna said I was a natural Spiritual Leader in step with the Creator and was indeed ready to carry this ceremony to others on my journey.

One sun I remembered that I had been thinking about going to the ocean. I asked Tuleco if he knew the way to get there. By now, I was used to having Tuleco around.

"The way to the ocean?" he asked, laughing. "I was born there. I did not come to Chi-Chen Itza until I was seven or eight summers. Yes, I know the way well, where to stop for water, to rest, where to find food, I even know how to fish and above all my family still lives there. Their village has no name but it is not hard to find. Many people go there because the fish are plentiful."

"Good," I said, "Get whatever we will need for the journey, we will leave soon."

I went to the Grand Chief's house to let him know of my plans. I found him having a session with four of the elders. I took them to be some of his advisors or intellectuals that he met with on a regular basis. When he saw me, he told the elders that he would return in a few moments.

When he approached, he had a frown in his face. "What is wrong?" he asked. Since I had been here, I never interrupted him in any way; he thought I was having some kind of problem.

"Nothing is wrong," I replied, "I only wanted to let you know I have decided to go to the ocean for a few suns to see if I can recall anything about my journey here."

"Good, good, go and enjoy yourself," he said laughing. "Take Pluma Rosa and Florecita with you to take care of you. They will pack a basket of food for you to take."

"I will not be needing them. Media Luna has sent me a young man to serve me. He will be enough help and my guide. He was born on the coast. He knows the area well."

I walked back to my quarters where Pluma Rosa and Tuleco were wrapping tortillas, goat cheese, and dried deer meat into a clean white cloth. Tuleco said we would not need water he knew where to get it, and we did not need to carry fruit, for there was plenty on the way. Everything was put into a woven bag with handles. It was woven from some kind of plant fibers.

Tuleco was a good-looking young man of sixteen summers. He was short, thin, but stringy muscled with long black hair, the front of it cut straight across his forehead just above his eyebrows. He had the strength of youth and the ambition of always wanting to do everything as quickly as possible. He was always looking over his shoulder to show off and let everyone know he was intelligent and ambitious. He would watch me trying to anticipate what I wanted or might need and try to get it for me.

At mid morning without anything else to keep us we set off. I tried to let Tuleco lead the way and he stepped close to me as we walked and quietly told me he could never walk ahead of me. It was not the way of his people. He

74

knew his place and always had to show respect and walk behind his master. I told him I was not his master and he was just my helper and could do as he wished.

He gave me a look that told me he appreciated what I said but he must always stay and not stray from his place in life. He would always be the one to serve someone; he had been born to do this. All this I could see in his eyes. The fatalism was that deep set in his features that it was unmistakable. That is the way it had always been and that is the way it would always be. He had been born a peon. That he had been allowed to serve Medicine people was a great privilege and honor for him. Above all that he had been very fortunate to be chosen by the spirits to come to help me, Kokopelli.

"How can I lead if I do not know the way?" I asked him.

He laughed and said, "Do not worry, the trail is easy to follow. If you do stray I will let you know with a whisper." He continued chattering, talking and laughing, showing the people they passed he was happy and had a good master. It also showed he was not beaten, nor afraid.

As we walked through the city, we encountered thieves, beggars, and women of easy virtues. Tuleco knew them all, most of them by name and told them not to bother his master for he was Kokopelli. It seemed that many had already heard of me, especially some of the young women, they tried to get my attention by winking at me and calling my name. I felt embarrassed and walked even faster. The people were parting, letting us walk through, where moments before it would have been almost impossible to fight our way through the crowds.

We finally left the crowds behind and moved on through streets with very few people on them. As we walked passed the last houses the jungle immediately took over the land.

CHAPTER 10

THE MAN IN THE MIST

The last houses, which seemed more like shacks than dwellings, slowly thinned out. Tuleco set a more leisurely but steady pace as we entered the thick jungle country. The trail to the ocean shore was easy to follow as it was well used. The thick, humid jungle was full of life. Birds of many different colors and sizes flew in all directions. Insects of every description and size scampered away at our approach.

I felt good. I was out of the small house and on the move. Walking and stretching my legs again was easy and comfortable for me. I pulled my flute strap off my shoulder and started to play. I played a happy tune keeping in step while I walked. I noticed Tuleco fell into step with my music. We walked and I played. We covered the distance quickly. My music seemed to draw animals and birds toward us and to the trail. It might have been only their curiosity, but it made our traveling more interesting.

Since everything I played, was played by whatever I was feeling. The music ended only when I grew tired and stopped. I slipped the strap back over my shoulder as we continued walking, content with life and where I found myself.

We traveled until the sun was directly overhead when Tuleco started to look for a small side path. The young man told me he knew of a very special place where we could stop, rest, and have our midday meal and siesta. Tuleco knew where the path was, but he also knew it was hard to find. Tuleco believed that the spirits would hide the path if they did not approve of the people trying to find it.

We walked by it after several tries before Tuleco found it. It was very well hidden in the thick brush. He called for me to follow him. I had to bend at the waist to get through heavy thick branches. On the other side, there was a clearing and a large statue of a huge head. It must have been a tribute to one of their Gods.

Tuleco told me he heard this was a holy place. It was where medicine priests came to do special ceremonies. That was long ago before his people were here and no one knew when that happened. He also told me many people were scared to come to this place, but he was not, only he did not think he wanted to spend the night there especially if he were by himself.

There was also a beautiful little spring bubbling out of the ground. The water was clear, delicious looking and ran for a small distance, disappearing into the underbrush. Tuleco put down the woven bags. One of the bags had the cheese and corn tortillas in it. The other bag Tuleco had brought personal things; I found out later he had gifts for his family.

He told me to relax and have a drink saying he would return in a few moments. He said he was going to see if he could find some fruit for our midday meal. He walked a few steps and the brush swallowed him as though he was never there.

I took my old robe off, which I now used as a pack for my back, and put it down. Then I removed my shoulder robe, laid it down next to the large sculptured head. It was so hot wearing only my breechcloth, felt good, comfortable, and much cooler. I walked to the spring and marveled at the beauty of the crystal clear water bubbling out of the ground. I knelt down, cupped my hands, and drank from the spring. After I had my fill, I splashed the cool water over my head and washed my face. It helped to refresh and make me feel better.

The water was as good as it looked. It was cold and sweet, but also had the faintest taste of minerals in it. To me it tasted much better with that in it. It reminded me of the springs in the desert from somewhere in my past. I could not recall ever seeing water bubbling out as fast as this one. I sat on the ground covered with short grass as though wild game grazed there. It seemed as though not many people knew of or came to this place. It was indeed special, and had a different energy from the trail we traveled getting here.

I rested my back on the face of the stone statue and listened to the jungle. I got an eerie feeling that either I was not alone or someone was looking at me. I looked around carefully getting an uneasy feeling. Yet, behind the apprehension I felt a comforting voice saying I had nothing to worry about.

No sooner had that thought registered, when out of the corner of my eye I saw what appeared to be a figure standing on the other side of the clearing. It was not very distinct and seemed to be made of smoke or a mist of some kind. The mist or was it a spirit, remained directly in front of me. It slowly materialized into what seemed to be a solid form. It was the body and appearance of a much older man. Like me, he had a long beard, mustache, and long hair.

Quietly I heard him say, "You should have more respect for other people's spiritual places." I took that to mean I was not to use the head statue as a backrest.

I apologized for my disrespect as I got to my feet and stood listening.

"We see that you have been busy. Busy learning the ceremonies, and passing knowledge on to those that need the wisdom you were given. You have also been busy with the women. Though you have treated them with respect, we want you to understand how sacred the pleasurable act of joining with a woman is. When you have that union with a woman, you are giving her the chance of becoming a life-giver. That is sacred. You must not take this lightly. Many women would not have been able to bear children in their present circumstances. You were made desirable to them to provide them the opportunity to become life-givers and bear children."

"Why was I chosen? How am I worthy of this special mission?" I asked the man in the mist.

"My son, you were selected because of the people and place where you came from. It was filled with spiritual people such as yourself and they were your relatives. You came into this world with their blood in your veins, and though you walk in the human world, you have one foot in the spirit world. You represent both the spirits and the humans. What you do is important, and you must never abuse or take for granted this path that is laid out for you."

I stood there unable to answer for a moment, my mind spinning. Finally I managed to stutter, "I am honored to have been picked for this and will do my best to fulfill all that is expected of me. I apologize for enjoying what I do so much, but I cannot help it, it is my human side. That does not stop me from being the spiritual person that I have to be to continue on this path."

"Do not misunderstand me, I do not expect you to go through these experiences without lust and love. This is how it has to be in order for you to produce what the women want and need from you. Continue as you have, if you stray or need our guidance again, we will come to you. We also want you to know that the people you are going to meet when you reach your destination need your help. They will need your advice and guidance, and that is what you will provide," his voice and image was beginning to fade.

I waited for more conversation from him and moved toward the mist to see if we could communicate more. As I got closer, the shape of the man/spirit dissolved and became a misty fog that drifted away into the bushes and low branches.

I stood for a few moments thinking of what I had seen and wondered if I had truly seen it or was it only my imagination. I looked around, found a large tree, and decided to sit against it instead of the large stone face.

I could hear many different insects making noises and rustling in the brush. I knew the ground and tree frogs made some of the noises because I heard them since I arrived in this country. It was surprising how some of the small frogs made more and louder noises than their larger friends.

As I sat with my back to the old tree I felt something uncomfortable prodding my back so I moved around to see what it was and to my surprise, it was a large piece of tree sap that was old and hard as a rock. It was so old that it was very dark, almost black. I did not know what it was but I had a strong suspicion that it might be Copal. I broke it off and placed it on my old robe.

It was odd that I had not noticed it before I sat down and leaned on it. I thought about it for a long while and thought if it had come to me without me looking for it, it was a gift from the Creator and I must use it in a good way. Since I was taking it, I must also give something in return. It was always good to stay in balance with nature and all creation.

Thinking of what I could give in return, I looked around asking myself that question. My eyes suddenly moved to and stopped on the woven bags Tuleco had been carrying. I got up, walked to them, and found the cheese and tortillas. I broke a small piece of cheese and wrapped it in a corn tortilla. I offered it to the four directions, to Father Sky, Mother Earth then placed it at the foot of the large old tree that had given me this wonderful gift.

I returned to the spring for another drink. I looked back to the tree and looked for the offering, I just made and it was gone. I could not believe my eyes. Either some small creature or the Spirits already took it. It made me feel good they had accepted my gift and had taken it so quickly. I was in balance.

I would ask Tuleco if it was indeed Copal and what he thought had taken my offering.

It was hot and still. The silence became a relaxant to me.

As the moments passed, I relaxed, enjoyed the fresh water, the jungle music made by the birds and the almost total quietness. I thought about the apparition I had seen and wondered what lay in store for me in the future. My eyes closing slowly I started to nod, overcome by the Spiritual feel of the place, the heat and the sound of the water coming out of Mother Earth.

The spell was broken when I heard a commotion in the brush. It was something big and it was coming toward the spring and me. Alarmed I jumped to my feet and faced toward whatever was coming. Tuleco stepped into the clearing. He was carrying Mangos and Papayas wrapped up in the cloth he used as a pack.

Over his shoulder, he was carrying a whole branch of small Platanos (bananas). It seemed quite heavy and caused the young man to pant from exertion. Getting his heavy load through the brush and trees had become a hard task. It had made him sound like a whole herd of large animals rushing through the underbrush. After putting the load down he smiled still breathing hard and told me that these small Platanos were hard to find where his family lived, so when he found the bananas he had to bring them as a gift to his family.

We ate like royalty that mid day meal. My young helper had found so much fruit in the jungle (selva) that we had more than we could eat. He said anything we could not carry we would leave beside the trail. Other travelers or animals would find and eat it.

Tuleco said that this would be a good place to spend the hottest part of the day before going on. He tried to convince me that it would be better for the two of us to rest. I on the other hand did not like to lay down with a full stomach. I decided that we would continue our journey.

I grabbed one of the woven bags over Tuleco's protests and told him we would continue. I wanted to get to the ocean before nightfall. Tuleco shouldered the branch of bananas and picked up the bag with the tortillas and cheese.

It took only a few moments to walk back to the main trail. When we had walked only a few steps and I turned to look back to where we had emerged and I could not tell where we had come out of the brush. The brush had closed up as though it had never been.

Thinking to myself, I wondered why we had gone there. Was it so I could see the man in the mist, and talk with him? I felt as though I was put in my place, but I did not feel as though I was scolded. That is when I began to just listen to my thoughts and stop trying to analyze every thought or occurrence.

We walked steadily for quite a while, until I began noticing Tuleco was starting to struggle to keep up with me with his load of bananas. He was beginning to tire, but would not admit it nor ask to stop.

"Is there a good place to stop, rest, and have a drink of water?" I asked him.

Pointing with his chin and puckered lips, he indicated that just beyond a big tree on the right there was another spring and shade.

Reaching the shade of the tree Tuleco set his load down and though his strength and youth were strong, it did have limits. I thought his living in the big settlement, not doing very hard work for the High Priest had not helped him stay in very good physical condition, and it was evident. I heard him sigh as he placed the stalk of bananas on the ground.

We both drank from the spring and for some reason I did not enjoy it as much as the water from the first spring. It did not taste as good.

I showed him the piece of sap I took from the tree and related how I found it.

He agreed that the Spirits might have brought it to me. He also said, "Men that looked for it had special ceremonies before they went to try to find it. They considered it a mystical gift from the Creator. They had to earn the right to search for it, but could not use it. They had to bring it back to the Medicine People for they were the only ones with the right to use it and only in ceremonies," He concluded, "I should consider myself very fortunate to have found it. Then again," he said, "you do have the right to use it. This is why the High Priest asked you to accompany him to the top of our most sacred pyramid. Common people such as me are taken to the top - only for blood sacrifices."

He also told me that if they have no enemies to sacrifice, some of the people from the village are selected for that purpose. It was considered an honor to be used in this way; the person that gives their life to the Spirits has his entire family looked after from then on. It is seen to it that they never need nor want anything for the rest of their lives.

"I see you have some different ways, and one of the reasons I am here is to teach love and compassion. I think I made a good start with Grand Chief Atoleh. I hope you will see some changes in the future," I pointed out.

Tuleco replied, "I have already noticed some changes, now I understand why and I am glad to see the changes you have started."

Our rest over, we were back on the trail moving toward the ocean. I wanted to see if I could recall how I had arrived to this land. I wanted to see if something made my memory return.

The shadows were getting long on the ground and twilight was beginning to take over the day. The night frogs were starting to sing their mating songs.

From far away first I started to smell the ocean then I felt a slight hint of a cooler breath of air touch my face. The air had a different feel to it and a very definite change was quickly taking place, as we got closer to the ocean shore. The change of cooler air felt wonderful after the humid heat in the jungle. I noticed Tuleco's step was picking up and seemed to get lighter the closer we got to his home.

CHAPTER 11

FIRST LOOK AT THE OCEAN

It was almost dark when we saw cooking fires in front of a cluster of small huts. I could see a few people moving between the fire and us. The surf was making its own music as it reached in to kiss the white sand and then gurgled happily as it raced back into itself.

Tuleco called loudly to his father. When they heard him it looked as though they had been startled. Everyone started running around frantically doing last minute chores and picking up things that needed to be put away. Then as a group, they came together and walked to meet and greet us.

There were three adult men, seven women, and several children. I found out later who they all were. Three of the women were the wives of the men and three were their daughters. The last adult woman was a widow of more than two summers.

My companion's father stopped in front of us and greeted us with warmth and respect. He told me he was called Pescado (Fish) because he swam like a fish. Pescado said they were waiting for us and honored to have me visit them.

He told me he had a gift for me and handed me a beautiful large seashell. It had all the outside cleaned off and polished to a shiny finish. It also had a landscape with a pyramid in the center sketched on the back of it. It was pink and light tan in color and I recognized it to be the same conch (shell) the men had used at the Temascal (Sweat Lodge) ceremony to call in the Spirits.

I thanked him profusely and told him I would use and care for it always. I marveled at its natural beauty.

He beamed with pride and told me he found it at the bottom of the ocean, brought it up and done all the work himself.

Again, I thanked him and told him he had done an excellent work of art.

I looked at Tuleco with a question on my face, asking him how they knew we were coming. He only shrugged his shoulders, as though saying he knew nothing.

With an attempt at making me welcome, his father, bent at the waist waved his arm toward the village with a flare, Pescado opened the way to their homes to us. As we walked to the huts and fire, the host told us that food and drinks were ready for us.

The children followed Tuleco because he had the sweet Platanos and other gifts with him. They went to one of the huts close to the fire. It was the hut where his family lived.

I was led to a spot where several large green leaves had been spread on the sand and made into a place to eat.

One of the girls waved to me to come to her, asking me if I wanted to wash myself. She was holding a large gourd with water. I nodded my thanks, put my old robe, woven bags, and flute down. I walked to where she stood and let her pour water over my head and face. I finished washing my face and beard when another of the girls handed me a long piece of cloth to dry myself.

Everyone had stopped before we arrived at the place that was set up for me to eat. I expected them to sit and eat with me and I was surprised when they declined. I was told that this food had been prepared especially for me. I felt uncomfortable and asked for Tuleco.

He came running and asked what was the matter. I asked if he was not going to eat. He replied that he could not eat with me. That would not be right for him to do so.

"It is not my place," he said. He also said that as a holy man I always had to be given every place of respect and privacy I needed or wanted. He wanted to eat and visit with his family if it was agreeable with me. If not he could sit close by in case I needed him.

"No, go eat and be with them," I said to him. "You must have much to tell them about the things you have seen, learned and done."

As soon as I sat down, I was given a gourd with fresh water to drink. Tuleco's younger sister, her name was Conchita (Little Shell) about fifteen summers, was the first to bring food to me. She brought a small clay pot with a fish soup. It had vegetables in it and of course, the always present, hot chili peppers. It was very chili and heat-hot, but also very delicious. Perhaps it was only because I was beginning to get used to eating the peppers and I was hungry.

Then one of the older women arrived carrying a long clay tray. She was about twenty-five summers and I found out later was the widow. On the tray were scorched leaves that were burned on the edges. She looked straight into my eyes. Her eyes were like black agates and beautiful.

Setting the tray down she carefully removed the leaves and inside to my surprise there was a large whole fish. The smell was wonderful and even though I had eaten the soup, my mouth started watering.

Carefully she reached over the fish using a long metal knife and a wooden spoon, peeled the outer skin back exposing the steaming white meat. The woman was very efficient at doing this for me, looking at me without speaking as though trying to give me a message.

Out of the folds of her dress, she pulled a small leather pouch that carried salt. Then she took a pinch of salt and spread it over the fish. Then from another pouch, she sprinkled fine ground chili powder lightly over the fish.

Conchita brought a plate of an oblong fruit that was green on the outside. She started to move around the older woman to set the plate down in front of me. The older woman stepped in front of her taking the plate and, making sure that I noticed, placed it within my reach. She smiled at me all the while using the same knife she sliced the fruit with many small black seeds. She called it a papaya. Having done what she could she stepped back to wait with the others. Out of the corner of my eye, I sensed Conchita glowering at her.

They all stood back, waiting for me to start eating. I looked around at them then lowered my head and said a prayer of thanks. Using my fingers, I took a bite of fish and put it in my mouth. It was so tender it dissolved easily and the taste was indescribable. I had never eaten such a wonderful tasting fish in all my days.

When they knew I liked it and approved, they all quietly moved away and back to their huts to eat and share together, leaving me alone to enjoy my meal. All except the older woman, I never noticed when they left.

Mid way through my meal, I picked up my cup to drink and it was empty. The older woman must have been waiting and watching me, because she immediately filled my cup from a clay pot. I looked up to thank her and was surprised at the open invitation on her face and eyes. Her sultry eyes were half closed as though already making love to me. It made me sit up and pay attention.

"What are you called," I asked her.

She replied in a beautiful husky voice, "My name is Estrella Blanca (White Star), but everyone calls me, Estrella."

"Thank you for your attention to me, Estrella, and that is a beautiful name." When I said that, I took a minute to look over her ample body and felt a stirring inside my loincloth.

I ate and drank the cool water until I could eat and drink no more. When I had my fill, I looked around. I could see some of the people by the firelight moving about, and some of them sitting and eating. I was happy to see they had enough to eat for I could see they were poor and had very little. The sea was their mother and their father, it provided for them well.

Estrella picked up the tray and anything left and took it with her, then walked away.

Now I was sitting alone with only the waves splashing on the sand and the stars as companions. I was full, content, and happy to be where I was at that moment. Where no one could see it, I felt an ache of loneliness deep inside. When I saw the men with their women and children sitting, eating, and quietly talking together, I felt the pain of loneliness deeply.

Then I realized being lonely was not what I was supposed to be doing on this journey. I sighed and turned my thoughts to the things that already happened to me. I also thought of what I would be doing while here on the shores of this beautiful ocean. I sat enjoying the warm quiet evening and the harmony made by the tree frogs, night birds, and the surf. I picked up my flute and joined the chorus of nature's music. Involved with listening and playing I did not notice the villagers were slowly gathering around me sitting down to listen.

When I did notice I smiled at them, singling each one in turn with a smile and a nod as I blew into my flute. I played for them just to watch their faces. It made me feel good to see them happy even if it was only for a short while. Sorrow seemed to be all over their faces. When we arrived the children stood sadly and quietly to the side trying to remain inconspicuous. Their sad faces making them look older than they were.

I finished playing and immediately Tuleco's father asked me if I was tired after such a long day. Acknowledging that I was tired, I stood up and gathered my robe and flute. He led me to a small hut that was some distance from the other ones. He had a clay urn sitting on the sand with a small fire burning inside of it for light. There was a piece of woven material stretched from one corner of the hut to the other. I did not know what it was until he spread and showed me how to get in. He called it a Hamaca (Hammock). He did not stay long just making sure I did not want anything else. As soon as he stepped out of the hut, he disappeared into the night.

I stood next to the Hamaca and dropped my clothes to the sandy floor. I spread the woven fibers and tried to get into it. It proved not to be as easy as Pescado had made it appear. After attempting to get into it, I succeeded on my second attempt. I lay on my back and slipped into a tired sleep. At first, I was very comfortable, then in my sleep I tried to roll over. I could not do it. The woven strings of the Hamaca would cling to my body and not let me move. I felt trapped. I spread it open and got out of it. I picked up both my robes laid them on the sandy floor and curled up to try to get back to sleep.

Just as I was drifting off, I thought I heard a soft rustling or some kind of faint sound. Being not quite awake, it took a moment for it to register. Something was moving outside my hut. I thought I heard another sound, as I lay there now very much awake. The small burning urn on the floor was almost out and giving off very little light. It was hard to see well. I heard the soft sounds getting closer and closer. I prepared myself to fight or run whichever was the best for me when the moment came. At least I am awake and can defend myself. It did not occur to me to get to my feet for I still laid on my side waiting.

Then to my surprise, Conchita stepped into the dim light. She looked so beautiful in that soft light. She was not what a person would call a very small or petite girl, but she was very young and vulnerable. She wanted to grow up; she wanted to be a woman.

She did not say one word but started to take her dress off by pulling it over her head. After it was lying on the floor she looked directly at me and still not talking she stood in front of me as naked as the day she was born. By now, I was sitting up paying close attention to what was opening up before me.

She slowly turned so that I could get a good look at what I was being offered and given. She had the body and beauty of youth. Her breasts were not large but stood proudly as if for my inspection. I could see her nipples were hard with excitement at what she was doing. Her body was curved in all the right places. Surrounded by the small girlish triangle at the center of her body where her legs came together. She was so young, beautiful, tender she made me catch my breath, and I felt my mouth get dry.

She finally spoke. "I have never shown anyone what I am showing you now," she said breathing softly. "I offer myself to you to use me as you want. I want to be a woman and to have a child. I am getting old and there is no one here that can make this happen except you. When we heard that you were coming," she continued, "We also heard that you were the bringer of babies. That all a girl had to do was sleep with you one night to get a child."

She started speaking faster when she saw me shaking my head to say no to her. She said that the word about my exploits in the big settlement had reached them days before and they all knew who I was and what I could do.

"Put your clothes back on," I told her. "I cannot make love to my new friend's young daughter with a clear conscience. I would be violating a sacred trust and I cannot do that. Not only that but you must experience love and life with someone closer to your own age. I am much too old for you to have an affair with and you are too young to be thinking of having a child so soon."

To ease her disappointment I went on to say, "You are a beautiful girl and will make someone a good wife someday," I told her to put her clothes back on and return to her father's hut before something happened and we both regretted it. Seeing her beauty, youth, and her way of standing, I had to tell her to go. I was telling her to go because I felt my manhood beginning to stir and was afraid I would weaken and betray my host and his family.

Pouting because she was not getting her way she stomped her foot on the sand and exclaimed that her mother had given Tuleco birth when she was one summer younger than she herself was now. Not only that, she said her moon cycle had been occurring for several seasons now and she was a woman that needed to become full. "Do you think my father and mother do not know I have come to you?" She asked me. "I have never had a man before and my privates are untouched."

"That may all be true and as it should be," I said, "But I am still tired from the journey. I need to rest and get my strength back before I think of doing anything. Put your clothes back on and go. I give you my word that I will think about what you have offered to me this night. It is an honor that you are offering me such a wonderful and beautiful gift. Give me a chance to rest and think. I will let you know when and if I decide to see you. Do you agree with me?" I asked her.

She nodded her head in agreement and tried to make herself look as sad as possible for my benefit. She wanted me to feel bad that I rejected her. I was too tired it did not work on me. The girl pulled her dress over her head, turned, and was gone.

94

A few moments passed then, everything was back to normal. Once again, I could hear the tree frogs, waves on the shore and the normal night sounds. I wondered if it had actually happened or had I been dreaming? I felt of my manhood and it was still proud, so I believed that the young girl had indeed been there in my hut.

It was now late and the moon, our Mother Earth's little sister, started rising over the eastern water, waves, and ocean. It made it possible for me to be able to see things much better. I was glad it had waited to rise now instead of rising when the girl was here. It might have made her too alluring to resist.

The moon has very powerful energy and makes us do things we would not normally think of doing. It has a way with humans much the same as our sexual emotions.

Lying down on my robes, I just got comfortable when again I heard a faint rustling just outside my hut. The clothes rustling had stopped and for some reason it felt different than from when Conchita had been here. I thought she was returning and now I might not be able to say no. The moon was up and the atmosphere felt different and somehow more intimate. Something changed my mood and charged the air.

A small and almost unnoticeable breeze stirred the leaves on top of the hut and brought with it a faint smell of wild flowers combined with a hint of wild mint. The faint noise, the charged air, and now this new scent made me sit up and look toward the front opening of the hut.

In the moonlight, I saw a woman completely nude step into the opening. I knew immediately that it was not Conchita.

It was Estrella Blanca.

She moved in to the hut as quietly and as quick as a panther. As though to let me know what I had already guessed she said in her now familiar husky voice, that it was Estrella.

I started to get up but she was too quick for me. She was kneeling at my side before I could move. She did not waste energy on being subtle. She leaned over me and put her passionate lips to mine. She was like a very thirsty person finding a coldwater spring. It was as though she was kissing me and drinking me to restore lost energy into her body. She displayed a wildness that reminded me of a hungry lioness.

The kiss lasted long enough for my manhood to rise again. I started responding to her affections and her actions. Before Conchita left, I had started to get excited and after making her leave I had an enormous energy pent up inside. I had rolled over and tried to get back to sleep. Now that Estrella was here, I was not very far from being ready to get excited again. I felt that I had left something unfinished or incomplete. From the long kiss and the touching tongues, my manhood had come awake with a roar. It was so hard it almost hurt, but it was a good, delicious hurt.

She pushed me gently down on my back, reached down, grabbed my manhood first with one then both hands, and exclaimed she was so happy she came to visit me. Still on her knees, she shifted so her face was close to my pubic area. She bent over me as her head went down she whispered it was too dry and she was going to get it wet. I was faintly surprised but not upset at this turn of events.

Her mouth was soft, wet, and warm. I had to concentrate to keep from going over the edge. It was so unexpected that it had aroused me enormously. After the initial shock, I settled down to enjoy what was happening. She knew what she was doing and how to do it. As she moved her head slowly up and down my erection she would let it slip out once in a while and take the opportunity to say little endearing things like, it is so good, or oh my it is so big. All those things that make men feel good.

It was feeling too good to me so I pulled her up into my lap. Without hesitation, she threw her leg over me and sat on my manhood. She let out a long sigh of happiness. She started slowly rocking back and forth. She would hold her shoulders still her hands gripping mine, moving only her pelvic area forward and back. It did not take long or much of this action to get us both to the top of the hill. We plunged together over the top and took a long while regaining our senses. She lay on my chest, both of us breathing hard.

With my manhood still proud, she sat up and started rocking again. This round was slower and in many ways more fulfilling. We took it easy and enjoyed every stroke of that satisfying love. Satisfied for the moment we lay next to each other, rested, and slowly regained our composure.

Then unexpectedly she jumped to her feet and grabbing my hands, she said that we should go to the ocean for a swim and to wash ourselves. I was hot from the exertion and hot from the heat and humidity so I got to my feet.

It felt good to be running naked and free on the beautiful white sand, on a clear moonlit night. When we reached the water, she ran straight in until she was far enough out to dive headfirst into the waves. I followed her until I was waist deep in the water. I did not go deeper; I did not know how to swim. She came out of the water and swam back to me urging me to go to her. I told her that I could not swim. When she got close to me, she hugged and kissed me. Then she said she knew of a good place where we could go and led the way.

We went to an outcropping of rocks and walked around them. There was a small pond of water. It was only waist deep. It was a beautiful place secluded, private, moonlit, and the water was warm.

We washed by scrubbing with the sand then rinsing with the clean water. We splashed around for a while until Estrella said she had to return to her hut before her aunt found her gone. Her aunt was very strict with her even if she had been married once.

As we walked back toward my hut we dried off and we started to talk. I told her I heard she was a widow and I asked what had happened to her husband.

She did not want to talk about him, so she shrugged her shoulders and said the ocean had taken him. He went fishing one day and never came back. That had been long ago and she wanted to feel alive like this night. Then she admitted that she had been on her way to see me when Conchita had arrived ahead of her. She had waited just beyond the light to see what I would do. She said she was glad I had sent her away and waited for her.

"I did not know you were coming and was not waiting for you, but I am glad you came to visit me." There were other things I wanted to know but did not feel she was the person to ask.

Arriving back at my hut, she quickly kissed me and without another word, she ran away toward her hut.

I walked in with a sigh, lay down on my two robes, and was instantly asleep.

The next thing I knew it was morning or so I thought. I sensed a presence in the hut. I opened my eyes to find Tuleco sitting just inside the hut. He was being very quiet not wanting to disturb me. I sat up and asked how long he had been waiting for me and if it was getting late. I got up while he was talking, tied my loincloth on, went outside, and relieved myself. I walked back in and sat on my robes.

He replied that he had only then arrived and that the day was half gone but it did not matter that we had nothing to do except rest, eat and relax. He walked outside and brought a soup pot with several large crustaceans (shrimp) already cooked and still hot. He added a pinch of salt and some dried ground chili peppers. He showed me how to eat them. They were very good. Tuleco said they were good and fresh as they had slept in the ocean the night before and caught that morning. He also had a large bowl filled with fruit.

He poured water for me to wash my hands and face. As I dried myself, I told him to go get his father and the other elders and tell them I wanted to talk to them. Ask them to come and eat with me. He left immediately.

When they arrived, they were all together. It was Pescado and two other elders. They stopped outside and did not want to enter the hut. Tuleco tried to get them to enter but they wanted to talk to me from outside. I had to get up, walk out, grab their arms, and pull them into the hut. They had grown up respecting and fearing anyone above their own peon status. I finally got them seated and relaxed. As we started eating Tuleco went to get more food. We ate without me saying why I wanted them and they did not ask knowing that I would talk when I was ready.

CHAPTER 12

TEMASCAL FOR THE COMMON MAN

When we finished eating, we walked outside and sat on the ground on the shade side of the hut. I began the conversation by asking them whom they prayed to. They looked at each other waiting for someone to say something. Then Pescado said they only worshipped the sun and the ocean. These two provide us with all our needs. The ocean gives us fish and we know nothing will grow without the sun so to us they are sacred. He finished by saying they only prayed when things were not going well.

"Is there no God for you?" I asked them.

They replied that only Medicine People had the right to pray to the gods.

"That is where you are wrong," I told them, "the Gods listen no matter who prays and respects them. It could be that is the reason why things do not go well for you. If you do not know how to pray to the Gods I will teach you, if you want me to."

They looked at each other almost in fear. Then one of the other elders said they would get into bad trouble with the High Priest. He also said the High Priest never came to their village, but some how the word would get back to him and there would be trouble.

Pescado said, "Forgive us for being afraid, but we never pray to the Gods together, it is only done by the priests."

They all sat back quietly waiting for me to say or do something.

Finally, I asked them if they would allow me to teach them, because I had the High Priest's permission.

"We have always wanted to do something like that but we fear for our families and ourselves," Pescado said. "As long as it does not bring problems to our village we will listen and try to learn."

They looked at each other, then all the elders agreed enthusiastically.

"Good," I said, "Prayers are for all of us. Are we not all God's children? I have found through the years that if you want things to go well for yourself, you must ask for yourself. I believe God helps those who help themselves. Let me help you and see what happens."

Then I stood up indicating the talk was over.

They all rose and thanked me for the meal as though I had provided it. I knew they were the ones who had been out fishing and finding the fruit I had eaten. After they left, I asked Tuleco how quickly he could get ready to go to the big settlement and how long it would take him to return.

I wanted Tuleco to ask the High Priest's permission to build the Temascal using what was available here. We could use the long reeds and brush to build it, but I wanted to be sure it was all right with Media Luna. I also wanted to know if it was acceptable for women to pray in the Temascal.

Tuleco said he could be ready to go immediately. As he turned to leave, he said it would take him two or three suns to go and return. He also said he would send his sister to take care of me while he was gone. I saw him stop briefly at his father's hut, then leave running.

I walked alone to the ocean to stand and gaze out at the water wondering how I had come to be here.

For three suns, I rested, ate, bathed in the ocean, and got acquainted with the villagers. I walked the shore for long distances and found the sand to be almost as fine and pure white as anything I had ever seen in my life. Estrella would join me on these long walks. I was grateful to share such beautiful sights with her. We saw the perfect smoothness of the beautiful shore. It was broken up by small shells, an occasional large beautiful conch and our footprints.

The water was also a thing of beauty. It seemed to be painted with different colors; from crystal clear on the sand, to light green, to a dark green, to a dark blue. I could count six or seven colors. I was glad I had the opportunity to see the beautiful picture painted by the Creator.

Strangers started arriving at the small settlement. They all came by to see me and ask my opinion or advice on different matters. They almost all brought me gifts. People were becoming more comfortable with me. They were learning that even though I was close with the High Priest, I was not a threat to them.

I was sitting on the ocean side of my hut and it was the evening of the third sun when Tuleco returned.

I had eaten but I could see he was tired and hungry. Never far, Conchita was close by. I called for her to bring food and water for her brother. It seemed she was ready because she immediately had food for him. We sat outside and Tuleco said grinning - he had good information for me.

I told him that I had waited this long and could wait until he was finished eating. He was indeed hungry. I did not see him take a single breath while he ate.

When he had finished, he sat back and told the whole story. He ran almost the entire distance and when he arrived, the High Priest was in ceremony and could not be disturbed. He told the priest he talked to that he had an important message from Kokopelli. The priest said he would tell Media Luna and Tuleco would be sent for when the High Priest was ready. It would not be until the next sun. Tuleco left to sleep for the night.

Early the following sun, he was called and explained to the High Priest what Kokopelli wanted. The High Priest listened, then told Tuleco that he had to pray about it and would give him his answer on the following sun after breaking his fast.

Early the next morning, Tuleco was called back to speak to the High Priest. Media Luna said he prayed about what Kokopelli asked. He was told by the Spirits that the Temascal was for all the people. It could be built in a way to make it available to anyone wherever it could be built. Kokopelli was to share everything he had learned in the last

103

moon with others so they might also worship the Creator. He said to tell Kokopelli that he had his blessings to go forth and teach what he had learned to those willing to share the knowledge.

It was good to have his blessing and permission. I immediately sent for the three elders of the village. I was amazed at how many others followed them. I did not realize how many people were now in the village.

When they arrived, we sat and talked about what was needed. I told them that the High Priest had a Temascal built of bricks and mud. "I see that you do not have those things available here. We now have permission to build it from the vegetation, saplings, and reeds available to us." That same afternoon we started to build it.

Everyone in the village turned out to help and see what was going on. So, we went about selecting the saplings. I noticed that more and more people were arriving and immediately started to help. Where I had told them the Sweat Lodge was going to be built, many of the women and children started cleaning the area. When I said I wanted stones, the young men asked what it was I wanted. I showed them. Many that just arrived went along the shore and started to bring back two and three stones at once. Soon they had a large pile of them ready to be used. Some were too small and some too large, but most were of a good usable size.

We finished the frame for the Temascal and as we all stood back to look at our work one of the elders said that it was not a castle but that it fitted them perfectly for they were poor and common men.

I told them it was as important and as sacred as any large pyramid or any place of worship for it was built with love and for the right reasons.

Then I asked for good dry wood, and as if by magic, a pile of wood started appearing. We laid some large logs on the bottom then placed the stones. It was burning fast and hot. Then I asked for blankets, cloth, or anything to cover the lodge. Several people went into the jungle and brought back large banana and palm leaves. They were perfect. The lodge was covered very quickly.

It did not take long before we were ready to have our first Sweat Lodge Ceremony. So, it happened that I started teaching and spreading the word of how the common man could have Spiritual cleansing, love, compassion, and the opportunity to pray.

I stayed on the coast for several moons and almost everyday new people would arrive asking for prayers and ceremonies. They would bring me gifts and their Spiritual pain seeking relief and comfort through prayers and sacrifice.

There was one occasion when a large storm arrived shortly after we had finished a ceremony. It blew away most of the huts on the ocean shore. All of us had to go inland for a long distance to get away from the rising ocean waters. Several villagers helped me carry all my belongings to a safe place. It rained like nothing I had ever seen and it did not stop for the length of three suns. On the fourth sun, the clouds moved on to the north and west. Grandfather Sun once more smiled upon us. As the water retreated to the ocean, we followed it. Many trees were broken and uprooted. Pescado said that the storm had come because we needed more firewood for the Temascal and for cooking.

With all of the strangers coming to the village, I noticed one young man, who had been in the Temascal, took an interest in Conchita. I noticed that she had not been around me as much as she used to be. One evening, I saw her and the young man walking away from the cooking fires, holding hands, deep in conversation. I was happy for her that she had finally found someone closer to her age and prayed she would find what she was looking for.

It did not take the people long to have my hut built again; they wanted me to have mine finished first. Then they quickly had their own huts built and ready to live in them. There was much vegetation and debris left on the beach. It was picked up quickly and burned. I was amazed at how soon after the storm they had everything back to the way it had been before the storm had come.

I asked Pescado about it and he told me that was the reason they built the huts from the trees around them. It was easy, available and they were used to doing it because these storms came every season.

The gifts brought to me were all very beautiful and at the beginning gave me a feeling of importance. One side of my small hut was full of gifts of all sizes and description, all of them handmade by people who were, "Of the Earth," as they called themselves. Some would bring me rings, bracelets, armbands, and necklaces made of a yellow metal. Some of the jewelry was of a white metal. The called the yellow metal Oro (Gold) and the white one Plata (Silver). They told me that both were very valuable and not easily obtained. Not many brought the metal jewels to me for they were poor people. I would look at my gifts with pride, they were all mine and I felt a strong sense of possession.

I suppose I was developing an ego because of the many gifts brought to me. What I thought of myself was beginning to interfere with my personality. I was beginning to let the respect and honor I was given, go to my head. Perhaps I was entitled to be treated in this way, but I certainly did not need to let it change who I was or what I was there to do.

I found myself thinking I was more important than what I truly knew I was - all because I was being treated with respect. I had people who followed me and wanted to learn from me. I could not see it until I recounted what happened at the small hut where I lived.

One night after a good hot Temascal, I had finished eating and was preparing for sleep when I felt a presence. I looked to the entrance of my hut and standing there was the same old man in the mist I had seen before. He was the one who appeared to me where we had stopped to rest. (This was where I was told not to use the large head as a backrest.) Now this man was much clearer.

He looked older than anyone I had ever met. He was rather tall but I could not see his feet and his head seemed to be touching the ceiling in the hut. His face was deeply etched with lines and small wrinkles. His eyes were deep, obsidian black.

Despite the lines, dark eyes and solemn look, he had a very calming and kindly face. However, all those things did not register right then.

I looked expectantly at his hands to see if he was bearing a gift for me. I now believe he saw the look of expectation in my face and eyes. He moved with an easy fluid motion into the hut. He sat on the sand pulling his robe around his legs. He did not exhibit the movements of an older man.

Then in a deep and strong voice, he asked me a question. It seemed to be coming from all around me, causing me to look all around the hut. Then he asked what I planned to do with all the things the people brought to me. Did I expect a gift from him as well? Before I could answer, he said he did have a gift for me. That it was indeed a gift, one he hoped I would treasure forever.

I told him these gifts to me were for the things I did for the people. I replied that I planned to keep them for they meant wealth, strength, and power. The gifts would give me the wealth to trade for the things I wanted to have.

"Have you ever considered that those things might not be gifts to you personally but offerings to the Creator," He asked. "Since you are his representative they bring offerings to you. You are allowing these offerings to sway your thoughts and eventually it will affect your Medicine and the power to help others. Although some of them are for you to use to ease your life, most are offerings to be passed on to those who need them more than you. You will receive so many offerings they will become a burden to you. The fact you are becoming accustomed to receiving things, does not speak very highly of you."

I asked him who he was. It felt strange for someone to speak to me with accusing words of wrong doings.

He explained, "My name is not important but who and where I come from, is. When you need to know I will tell you. For now you only need know that I came to help you."

I sat back in shock, for I thought in all my wisdom that I had been doing what I was there for and that I was doing a very good turn for the people.

As if reading my mind he said, "Yes you have been doing the work you were chosen for, but now you are allowing your human traits to cloud your spirituality and better judgment. God the Creator only wanted us to have a conversation to let you know there are many pitfalls on this path and you have found the first one. The choice is ultimately yours to pick your own path follow it to the end and accept responsibility for your actions. My job is to let you know that you are straying. Always be careful of your choice for the rest of your life will be influenced by your actions and decisions, right or wrong.

I want you to think about one other question I have for you," He continued in a slightly louder voice, "JUST how much do you NEED to live comfortably?" The words were sharp, designed to get my attention, and they did. They hung in the air like a thick clasp of thunder.

Sitting in awe of such a wise man was almost unbelievable to me and I was frightened. He must surely be a messenger from God. The warmth and kindness in which he had corrected me did not upset or make me feel like a failure. It made me more aware of my responsibilities to the people who believed and trusted in me. There was a special energy and strength about him.

He asked me what I wanted to do, that I had to make my choice now, to follow the path of material possessions or the Path of the Spiritual Warrior.

I replied that the Spiritual path was the one I had always wanted and that he was right. My thoughts and my mind were clouded with material things. I would gladly give away all the things brought to me if I could do it without hurting the people that brought them.

He said he was glad I made the Spiritual choice because that was where I was needed and where I would be the happiest. As for the things given to me he said, "Every fourth Temascal have a giveaway. Give the gifts to the people who need them the most. Always make certain that you do not give it back to the same person that presented it to you. If you do this by mistake, tell them that the gift has returned to them because they will need it in the future."

"By giving away all these wonderful gifts you will become known far and wide as the bringer of beautiful gifts, bringer of children, the bringer of sexuality and many creative ideas back into the lives of people who believe in you. That, my son, is the gift I have brought to you, the ability to help them in many different ways." He stopped talking and sat quietly as though in deep thought.

"One other matter that I want to talk to you about is your relationships with women," he said.

"Am I doing something wrong?" I asked.

"No, no," he answered. "There is some concern that you might hurt someone by your actions without knowing you are doing it. So far, you have only acted as all humans act and that is acceptable. You should be proud that you showed restraint with the young woman who offered herself to you when you first arrived here. Bear in mind that you must never under any circumstance take advantage of any female because of her vulnerability. Do not ever hurt or force any female to have a relationship with you. Protect them if you see someone trying to do wrong to them. The act of one person forcing himself onto another is going against the laws of God. That is something else for you to teach others. You are walking a very narrow path my son. Beware you do not fall off."

I thought I heard a sound at the entrance and glanced to it. There was nothing. I looked back to him, and to my astonishment, he was gone. It was as though he had never been. The odd thing about it all was that I looked at the place where he had been sitting and the imprints of his rear and sandals were still visible in the sand. As I sat there looking at them they slowly filled in by sand. Outside I heard the rustle of the palm leaves as though a slight breeze was stirring. Later I put things together and thought that it must be his spirit leaving.

I sat there for a long while thinking of what had transpired and felt humbled by the occurrence. Tears came into my eyes thinking of what I had almost lost because of my ego and greed. I let my ego get the best of me and was properly put into my place. I felt bad because I allowed myself to become someone I was not in my own mind. I made a promise to myself not to ever let myself do that again. I had put myself on a pedestal and had promptly fallen off.

For many suns, we had ceremonies every evening. There were always new people coming to take part in the lodges. I started giving away the gifts given to me. I always would look at peoples' eyes to see how they looked when looking at the gifts that lay on the floor or hung from the walls in my hut. I would present those gifts to them at the end of the ceremony. They were like children filled with happiness that I would seem to know what they needed.

Some evenings after ceremonies, I would sit close to a fire, and quietly play my flute. It became a gathering place for everyone enjoyed listening to me play. Some songs would be sad and heartfelt while others would be light-hearted and happy tunes for the children. It seemed that I could always look up and see Estrella sitting and smiling at me. Her aunt could be seen now and again enjoying my music. I felt that this was another one of my gifts to give them.

CHAPTER 13

ANOTHER KIND OF LOVE

Early one morning I walked to the place I thought of as my sanctuary, a private small space on the shore, the place Estrella had shown me when I first arrived. When it was known that it was where I preferred to go to be alone, very few went to that place so I could have my privacy.

Occasionally late in the darkness after a Temascal, I would go there to bathe and cleanse myself. When I felt the need I would give Estrella a special look and she would know to come to me. She also knew to be very discreet about getting there. Estrella would not come unless I gave her the sign. It was very refreshing there as the nights were always hot, so the cool waters of the ocean were pleasant to my body.

One evening, after I had eaten, and gone to my special place, Estrella brought me a beautiful gift and this was indeed a gift, for I kept it and used it for many seasons.

We had both walked into the placid warm water and were beginning to enjoy ourselves. Holding something in her hand, she stood close to me and told me she had a small gift for me.

She handed me a soft beautifully tanned small deer hide. I could feel something slender long and hard in it. I thanked her for the gift and started to lay it on top of one of the large rocks that formed the pool where we bathed.

She stopped me and said that I must look at what she had given me. She said she had a very talented craftsman make it especially for me. She also told me to be very careful with it for it was delicate, very sharp and could be dangerous. I could see she was very excited to have me see the gift.

I nodded and holding it very carefully, I slowly unwrapped the gift. It was a beautiful long knife made of a black but translucent piece of stone (obsidian). It was as long as the end of my middle finger to my wrist. Somehow, the craftsman had sharpened it so all I had to do was slide it across something and it would be cut. I experienced it immediately by sliding it across my thumb and making a small cut on it. I learned to respect it right away.

"Why do I need such a sharp knife?" I asked her.

She knew she could touch me because of our shared intimacies. What she wanted to show me was something different. She waded close, put her arms around me in a

113

warm embrace, and put her head on my chest. She held me there for a few moments then slowly reached up and touched my face where my full beard was dripping water.

"Have you ever thought of removing your face hair?" She asked me, as she ran her hand through it. It was quite long and reached down to my chest.

"I have cut it before when it was too long or when it became bothersome, but I have never given it much thought," I replied.

"With this knife you can cut it close to your skin," she told me, "It would not be so hot for you under all that hair. The air can touch your skin and refresh you. Most of our people have very little face hair because we pull it off. With as much as you have it would be better to cut it, than to pull it off. It would not be so painful."

"I would not care if it was on or off," I said. "Would you prefer if it were cut off?" I asked.

She replied that she would like to see what I looked like without it.

I told her that if she could do it I would let her. I could not see what I was doing and I would rather not cut my face by attempting it myself. If I did not like it, it would grow back later. She was right it was hot under all the hair.

She said she had never cut hair like this before but if I stood still she would be very careful and do it for me.

Still standing in the water she pulled me to sit on a large rock that was half in and half out of the water. She had come prepared. In a small piece of cloth, she had a piece of the same kind of root that the two girls had used to wash me before. As she rubbed it on my face, it did not foam up

114

as much as it had before but it helped my face hair soften and cut without as much trouble.

She asked me to lie back on the rock and she took the knife and slowly started scraping from my neck up toward my chin. For a brief moment I felt a chill and my body was covered with bumps. I thought of Media Luna and the sacrifices he performed with a knife like this one.

The knife was so sharp that the hair came off my neck very easily and without any discomfort. When she started on my face, she first grabbed handfuls of the long hair and cut it short. Then she wet and rubbed my face with the root again. Very carefully, she slowly brought the sharp stone knife down and close to the skin without cutting it. She was very intent during the entire process. Finishing one side of my face, she worked on the other. On my chin, she was even more careful. She looked at my mustache and said that was enough. That it looked good and would leave it, but she did cut some of the length to keep it out of my mouth when I ate.

She pulled me to my feet and stood looking at me very seriously, and then she smiled and pulled my hand to go to the top of a large rock that had water in it. In it, I could see my reflection. I was surprised at how different I looked without all the face hair. My face was very pale.

As we talked about my new look, we both walked naked, back into the warm pool to continue our bath. Stepping in the water, I noticed it was twilight. Grandfather Sun was finishing his journey as Grandmother Moon was beginning hers and she was complete (Full Moon). I knew that for Grandfather Sun and Grandmother Moon to share the same sky was indeed a good omen. In most of the seasons, they were far apart. I felt it was a sign for special things to happen. Perhaps it was a sign to share love and affection with others.

Estrella Blanca said that she liked me much better that way, but I would have to get some sun on it so it would not be so white. It became part of my ritual. Once every seven suns I would scrape my face free of my facial hair.

She stepped up close to me again and held me in a strong embrace. She started pulling me back to the large rock where I had laid when she cut my face hair.

She was talking to me quietly with her face against my chest and her hands rubbing my manhood. It was starting to respond as we moved slowly through the warm water. I could not hear what she was saying and it did not seem to matter. What she was saying were just words of endearment.

When her back touched the large rock, she asked me to help her sit on it. Putting my hands around her slender naked waist made both my erection jump and my throat constrict. For a moment, I could not catch my breath.

Sitting up on the rock, she was holding my head to her breasts. She said, that she had been thinking a lot of me especially since it had been so long since we last made love. Now she was ready.

She had always been a bit aggressive, but I never minded her being like that. I let her take the lead and tell me what she was thinking and wanted to do. She was always thinking of different ways we could make love. I knew we were going to make love but what she planned surprised me, but not enough to kill my expectations.

She moved my head so one then the other of her nipples were hard with excitement. They went into my mouth. Of course, I had to do my part. I took her beautiful, dark, brown nipples into my mouth and gently sucked on them. I pulled them clamped between my lips and ran my tongue over them. When I did this I could tell Estrella was enjoying it for I could hear her soft moaning and long sighs. Then she put her mouth close to my ear and whispered that she was dry down there would I wet it for her as she had made mine wet.

It took me a moment to understand what it was that she wanted. I pulled back away from her, and then looked at her intently. I said I had never done that before and did not know if it was something I wanted to do.

She replied that she had never done anything like that either but for me she would do anything. She encouraged me to go on and do it, for it was only making love to a person you feel very close to.

Then I looked up into the sky and saw both heavenly bodies of Grandfather Sun setting, and Grandmother Moon rising. And then I thought about what I felt about loving to the fullest and that convinced me more than anything else, to do what I could and do it to the best of my ability.

I hesitated, but with her pubic hair and privates only a hands length away from my face and my excitement at the highest, I thought to myself that I would try and if it did not feel right I could always stop.

She laid back on the rock and waited her legs together. I leaned my head forward and tasted her. She tasted salty from the ocean water, but it was pleasant. To make it easier for me she opened her legs wide, putting the bottom of her feet together. I touched her gently with the tip of my tongue. I tasted and smelled a faint musky female scent that aroused me even more. I touched her again with my tongue and I felt her quiver. Apparently, I had touched something special. I touched it again and her whole body shivered. I had learned something new, that she was very sensitive in certain places.

Thinking of the many occasions that she had given me pleasure and served me hand and foot, I thought that this was little enough for me to do to pleasure her.

I found the experience helped to keep me highly excited also. I kissed her over and over until she almost jumped off the rock. Then her whole body became hard and stiff, as she let out a long and deep almost unearthly moan. I understood I had taken her over the edge, where I now needed to go.

Recovering slowly, she opened her eyes, looked at me lovingly, and said it was my turn to get on the rock. As she slid in the water in front of me, I was sticking straight up waiting for her. Instead of getting on the rock, I just picked her up and cupping her buttocks in my hands, I impaled her right where we stood, waist deep in the warm water.

I was so excited from what I had just experienced that my journey over the top was fast, long lasting, and deeply gratifying. After that, we lay on the soft sand and lazily watched Grandmother Moon walk across the sky for a long while. Then slowly we got up, embraced, and walked back to my hut like two new lovers.

After she left to go to her hut, I laid down trying to go to sleep. Thoughts of what we had just experienced together brought a new strange feeling in my heart. I felt as though I wanted her with me always. I wanted to protect her, watch over her, and share my life with her. Was I in love with her? Would I be able to leave without her? The way I felt, right now, I would want her to go with me, but the path I had to walk was not a path to share with her. The thought of her not traveling with me, made my heart ache. I lay there in confusion, attempting to think of everything, until sleep came.

When Grandfather Sun rose the next morning, word had spread that I cut off my face hair and people were starting to come and see me. They all made different excuses why they were coming to see me, but I knew it was only curiosity and I just enjoyed their attention.

Many of the villagers commented on my looks and said they liked it better that way. I do not know if they indeed liked it or if they were only saying it to please me, since it was already off and could not be replaced.

CHAPTER 14

RETURNING TO THE PYRAMID

One morning, not long after Estrella and I were together, I knew the moment had come for me to leave. Just thinking about it brought a pain in my chest and a lump in my throat.

Estrella and I shared so much since I came here, yet I knew she could not go with me. I knew the path chosen for me would not be a good one for a woman. Women need roots and a home – two things I would never have nor could ever give. I would not ask her to go with me for her own good. I also knew she would never ask to go with me if I did not ask her.

I felt I helped these people by the ocean as much as I could and must be on my way to help others and see different country. I decided to return to the large city where I first arrived. I spent the whole sun resting, then called Tuleco and Pescado, his father to tell them of my decision.

They tried to talk me into staying longer by saying the people needed me and they would be heartbroken if I left. I told them my mind was made up. The Creator was telling me to go. I also told them that had been the reason I conducted so many Temascal ceremonies for them, so they could conduct the ceremonies themselves. "Besides," I said to Tuleco, "if I did not follow what the Creator was telling me to do then I was doing the wrong thing."

Finally accepting they could not change my mind, they relented and wanted to go to tell the people. I told them to keep it to themselves and to help me with getting everything ready to go.

Right away, although they had told no one, the people knew there was something different amiss or something was wrong. The villagers started gathering around my hut. Then some started bringing food. The mood was somber yet there was also a happy energy in the air. It was beginning to acquire a festive mood. I thought that in their

120

own way they were trying to say they were grateful for me having spent some of my life with them.

As the people gathered and children played, some of the men wanted to have a special last Temascal. They realized what we were doing in getting me ready to go. Later we did have one last ceremony. After, I had the largest give away of them all. I gave gifts to all the men, women, and the children. I still had quite a few gifts left that I put into my old robe.

Late that evening well after Grandfather Sun was asleep, I lay down on the soft sand and tried to sleep. My mind was filled with thoughts and I kept questioning myself. I wondered if I was doing the right thing. I asked the Creator to tell me again if this was what I was supposed to be doing. Was I abandoning them? Restless, I got up to walk to my special place.

Standing by the pool in the moonlight was Estrella, gazing sadly into the water. I came up behind and put my arms around her waist. I noticed her stomach was larger than normal. I asked her what was wrong. She said sadly, that though she knew I must go, she felt a deep emptiness in her heart. She was happy, because she would always have a part of me with her in the child that was growing inside of her. I stood in shock and said I did not know what to say or think. I told her that I indeed loved her, and because of that, I could not take her with me. My road and path would be very difficult, hard, and lonely. I must go alone on this path. I felt a lump in my throat and the beginning of tears in my eyes.

She saved me having to explain more by taking my hand and pulling me back toward my hut. Reaching my hut, she let go of my hand and walked to hers. I closed my eyes sadly, and the tears finally rolled freely down my cheeks. Lying down I felt lost and alone. Sleep was the only thing to save me from the sad thoughts going through my mind.

By morning, I had my answer and knew my chosen path was the right way for me to go.

When I rose, it was still dark. Tuleco was all ready waiting for me with a cup of warm chocolate and the bags ready to be picked up. As I sipped the drink, first one torch was lit then another and another until several were burning, lighting up the entire area.

Everyone was saying farewell to me and trying to touch me. I felt so good for they had all become my family. I felt at first a small lump in my throat then it became bigger. I tried to laugh it off but it did not go away. As I started to feel tears building in my eyes, I tossed the gourd cup on the ground and before anyone could see my eyes, I said gruffly to Tuleco that we were leaving.

My answer was that as much as I had grown to love them and they to love me they were willing to let me go to do what I was supposed to be doing. Everyone was happy and comfortable with me following my direction. I believed that was my answer.

I picked up my old robe and put it over my left shoulder. It still had many things in it. The weight made me bend at the waist and lean forward, making me walk as though there was something wrong with my back. It made me walk like a hunchback. I put my flute to my lips and played a happy song as we walked away. Once I looked back and could see Estrella standing close to one of the torches, looking sadly. Smiling she waved with one hand, the other on her stomach. She seemed at peace with my leaving

Tuleco picked up the other woven bags and we started out. The villagers followed us for a distance. Slowly they started dropping back by ones and twos returning to the village until Tuleco and I were finally walking alone. From a far distance, I could still hear faint voices yelling farewell to me and to please return again.

We walked long and fast until we reached the place, where the large head and the clear running spring were found. Once again, we had to look hard to find the overgrown path that led to it. The water was as cold and refreshing as I remembered. We only remained long enough to drink and eat some of the tortillas and beans we had from the ocean village. I wanted to reach the large settlement before dark.

We continued in the hot and humid afternoon. I played my flute keeping in step with our strides. The flute music was a happy tune that reflected my mood. I was happy to be returning to a place of many pleasant memories. By early evening before Grandfather Sun went to sleep in the mountains to the west, we started encountering people moving in different directions, going about their chores.

Tired from our fast and long walk we passed the large pyramid. Stepping around crowds of people we went to the dwelling of the Grand Chief. When we arrived there was no one outside to talk to; we went on to my small hut at the rear of the enclosure. The coolness from the trees and running water was pleasant.

I went into the small room where I always slept, placed my old robe with the gifts that I brought back with me on the floor. I removed my other robe and walked into the room that had the bath and running water. Stepping into the fresh warm water felt so wonderful I almost fell asleep as I lay soaking my tired body.

I did not notice but Tuleco had gone to the main house to announce my return. My moments of quiet were suddenly broken by a rush of bodies all trying to get through the doorway at the same instant. Immediately the bathhouse was filled with four chattering, talking, and giggling girls. They were telling me they were happy I was back and that I looked strange without my face hair. They were all talking at the same moment and it was difficult to tell who was saying what.

They were anxious to tell me different things. Florecita, not having the opportunity to talk to me, said she was going to bring me food and that I must be hungry. All the other girls responded as one, exclaiming they also wanted to bring food.

When Florecita stepped outside she immediately flattened herself against the wall. The other girls, not to be left out of doing something for me followed Florecita at a run. Thinking she was ahead of them in the dark, they ran even faster and rushed right by her. As they all ran out saying they would also bring food, Florecita stepped back into my room locking the large wooden door latch. She walked into the bathhouse and said they could get the food; she would rather give me a bath.

She took off her dress and stepped into the bath water. She looked as beautiful as ever. Though I knew I could have her if I wished, I told her all I wanted was her company. I was too tired to think of anything else.

She found one of the scrub pads that had the yucca soap in it and started washing me from my head down. She stopped to look at my face. She would cock her face to one side then the other. Finally, she nodded her head and said that she liked me better without my face hair. Whomever the girl was that talked me into cutting it off, Florecita was glad. Then she asked coyly, if the girl was as pretty as she was.

I replied that she was as pretty but a much older woman. She was happy and satisfied with my answer. I could almost hear her saying that an older woman would not be a serious competitor. Little did she know how deep my feelings were for that "older woman."

She washed my privates and laughed when my manhood started to react to her gentle and soft hands. I slowly pushed her hands away from that sensitive area.

She asked me to sit up on the edge of the bath. She said that since my feet had carried me all the distance back from the ocean, they must be tired and she would massage them for me. My feet were sore until she started to softly manipulate them. At moments, her massaging was soft and at other moments, she put heavy pressure on them. My feet felt wonderful with someone giving them such good and loving care.

With my bath over, I sat and ate some wonderful food the girls had prepared for me. Tuleco stayed around waiting to see if I might need anything. Finished with my food and going to my room to lay down, Florecita followed me in.

She again asked if I needed her to stay. I told her that she should go and get a good night's sleep, for I would need her when Grandfather Sun awakened the following morning. I was very tired and all I wanted now was to sleep. Sadly, she bid me a good evening and left.

I had ended the sun long journey freshly bathed, a full stomach, and a good feeling of contentment. I could think of no better way to end a long trail.

I laid down and slept deeply. In my sleep, I dreamt that a girl came into the hut and was talking to me about the ocean. In the dream, it was a girl that looked like Pluma Rosa but was actually Estrella. She had her back to me and the person I touched, as I put my arms around her, was much thinner.

In my sleep, I pulled her very close and I started to feel excited. My manhood began to grow and expand. It went up between her legs from behind. My dream was so real that I could feel the body next to me. Asleep and feeling excited I let my hands move and touch her body all over. My hands went to her breasts and even in my dream, it did not feel right, but it did not register. Then my hands moved down to her front to her female parts.

What I touched there startled me and I was instantly awake. The moonlight was streaming through the open doorway. In my arms was Tuleco.

I was shocked and for a moment, I could not find words. I realized why even in the dream things did not feel like they should have. I swiftly got to my feet and saw Tuleco was awake also.

Trying to get control of myself for I was still sexually excited and confused, I quietly asked him what he thought he was doing and why he laid down beside me as he had.

He said that when he was told that he was to help me, it was to help me in all ways, not just to carry and get things for me. He belonged to me and I could use him anyway I wanted to, even this way.

I was shaking my head as he was talking. "Have I ever displayed or shown a desire to use you in this way?" I asked him.

"No, Kokopelli," he answered, "You never have, but when you told the girl to go I thought it was a good opportunity to demonstrate to you my willingness and love to do anything for you, even this. I feel in my heart, though you have said nothing about it, you will be leaving here soon, and I want to go with you. That is the reason I offered myself to you in this very intimate way. I want to show you that I can serve you in many different ways."

Slowly I replied, "I am truly sorry this has happened. I do like and respect you and I thank you for thinking that much of me to offer yourself as you have done. I do not want you in that way and now it has happened I would feel uncomfortable if you traveled with me. In my vision, I have never seen nor had anyone else with me. I must travel this path alone. It is my destiny," I said. "I must decline your offer, but I would like to always think of you as my friend if you will allow me."

Tuleco would not look at me as he nodded his head. "I have always looked and served you with love and respect," He said sadly, "Which is what you have taught me in the Temascal Lodge, but I guess I carried it a step too far. I did not think of the consequences. I apologize to you and hope you will forgive my lack of wisdom in that respect."

Feeling normal again, I looked at him with renewed respect for his confession and courage to express himself. I grabbed both his arms and pulled him to his feet. I embraced him and then held him at arm's length.

Warmly, I said, "No one ever needs to know this happened and that you are a true friend. Now, return to the High Priest and tell him I will see him after breaking fast in the new sun," I continued, "I will give him a good report on how you helped me and that you have learned much about the Temascal."

He left me standing there looking as he walked away. He was not his usual happy self. He turned and said to me, "It is not important if others hear what happened this night, for it has happened in the past. All my friends know this of me. In fact, there were several others like me helping the priests. I am not ashamed of who or what I am." With that said, he disappeared into the dark.

I felt sad because he had been a great help and good companion to me. I never saw him again.

At the beginning of the next sun, I awakened before Grandfather Sun had risen. I was having a hot cup of café when the Grand Chief's wife had me called to the main house. I took the opportunity to look through my old robe to find gifts. I found the largest, heaviest bracelet and most beautiful necklace I had and put it into my, now clean, robe. Someone had washed it for me the night before.

As one of the girls escorted me, she whispered Florecita was with child. I stared at her as though she had just grown another hand on her forehead. I did not have an opportunity to say anything before we arrived at the Chief's home.

"Sit," she said pleasantly. "My husband, the Grand Chief is away. He said if you returned before him, I was to ask you to tell me of your adventures while on the coast and what you have seen. He wanted to know if you figured out how you arrived here from the East."

While we talked, she had food brought in so we could break our fast and relax. She asked me many questions and wanted to know everything. Of course, I could not give her all the details. Nor did I tell her about the visit from the man in the mist and how he had made me realize what I was doing. I did tell her I had not figured out how I came to arrive there.

After answering as many of her questions as I could, I told her that I had been thinking of her and the Grand Chief. I brought them each a small gift. Her face lit up with excitement at the mention of a gift. She was like a small child waiting with anticipation as I searched through the folds of my robe. When I said I had found it, she leaned forward and almost fell out of her seat.

The bracelet was shaped like a serpent. The head had two small green stones for eyes. It was made to wrap around the forearm of the person wearing it. It was as wide as my small finger and quite heavy. She cried happily when she took it and thanked me. She asked me to help her put it on. When I said I had no idea how to do that, two of the girls that served us stepped in to help her.

"This," I said, "Is what I brought for the Grand Chief."

From the depths of my robe, I pulled out the large heavy necklace. It had large blue (azurite) and green (malachite) hand polished stones that had been perforated and strung on a hand made chain. Every link was of the yellow (gold) metal. Between each of the stones, it had four large solid round beads of the same metal.

"It was brought as an offering by one of the men that journeyed many suns from the south just to attend our Temascal. He remained several suns to learn the ways so he could go to his village and help others." I told her all these things as a way of giving her a little history about the gifts I brought them.

"I wish the Chief had been here to accept his gift," she said, then continued, "But you will see him after he returns and I am sure he will want to thank you personally."

"When will he return?" I asked her.

"He left only three suns before you arrived and he will not return for perhaps another moon."

"I am afraid that I will be gone by then," I said. "I feel I must move to on to help others. I will be leaving as soon as I am ready so I want to bid you farewell now. I truly feel I have found the wisdom I came here to learn. The things I did for the past moons while by the ocean was only to get the experience I need in the future. The moment has come for me to travel and teach others what I have learned."

She made a small sound of dismay and said she hoped I could remain longer, but understood I had visions and dreams. That is what I should follow. She also told me to be very careful as I traveled for it was a hard land and many would kill first before asking or knowing anything.

I bid her farewell and thanked her for all they had done for me. I turned and left her sitting there looking after me.

When I returned to my hut Florecita was there waiting for me. I did not know if what I was told about her was true. "Are you with child?" I asked her.

She bowed her head as though ashamed and replied that she thought she was because she had not had her moon cleansing since I left.

"Do you believe it is my child?" I asked her.

She replied, "You are the only man I have been with for many moons. Yes, I am certain you are the father of my child. Two other girls you slept with are also both with child. They are busy now and could not come to see you."

I was speechless for a few moments and told her I did not know what to say or do about it. I told her that I had many places to go and people to help. I held up my hands in a helpless gesture for her to see. I did not know what to do about this situation. .

She quickly reassured me that it was fine and truly her choice. She had wanted a child from me and I need not worry. The child would be well taken care of and never be in need of anything. The other two girls have asked me to tell you they expect nothing from you, they have what they wanted. It was I, that had given them the most precious of gifts, their infants. Then, in a very practical way, she asked if I needed help getting ready to go.

I do not know how, for I told no one except the Grand Chief's wife I was leaving; yet, everyone seemed to know.

I replied, "There is not much to get ready. All I will be carrying is the few gifts I still had left from before and a little something for me to eat on the trail." I heard someone ask for me by the main front entrance. I stepped out of my hut to encounter a young man that was panting from running. What is the problem, I asked him as he stopped in front of me.

He told me that the High Priest Media Luna wanted to see me before I left and asked if I could stop at the main pyramid and see him. I told him to let the High Priest know that I would be there soon, for I was almost ready to travel.

Before leaving my sleeping quarters I searched in my robe for some gifts, I might give to the girls I thought might be having my child. I found each of them a gold ring and bracelet. I knew they had some value. I did not know then, that only wealthy or important people wore any type of jewelry. I gave Florecita her gifts, kissed her gently on her forehead, and said farewell.

I started walking toward the main entrance and to my surprise almost all the help from the Grand Chief's household were standing by the entrance. They were all quietly waiting for me to go. The girls I had relations with were standing in front of everyone else, waiting and looking at me. When I reached Palomita and Pluma Rosa, I stopped and gave them a small embrace. I held their hands, and wrapped their fingers around the gifts. Beginning to feel lonely, I felt a catch in my throat as I bid each of them a quiet farewell.

I walked away hurriedly not wanting them to see my sadness. I was also feeling a tickle in my nose. It felt odd that I had only known these people for a brief period, yet felt as if I was leaving my birth home and blood family. I felt a great sadness and a heavy heart.

To try to make myself happy and anyone else listening, I put my flute to my lips and started playing a happy tune as I walked away as though I had not a worry in the world or tears in my eyes. I was still playing my flute to announce my arrival. At the foot of the great pyramid, I saw Media

Luna waiting for me. I was surprised when he greeted me warmly and with an embrace. He held me at arm's length as though I was his long lost son.

"I am proud of what you have done on the coast," he told me. "I received reports on how you ran the Temascal ceremonies and how the people reacted to your teachings. Do you know you are the very first person I taught and allowed to go forth and teach all that I have shown you?" He asked me.

I only bowed my head to acknowledge his words. I thanked him for letting me learn the Ways of the Temascal and granting me permission to help others. Though I knew he would or could not refuse me, because of him thinking I was a God, I still thought it was good to give thanks.

"It is not only what you have learned from me that is important. It is also important what I have learned from you. I have given much thought to the things you say in the Temascal. I have listened to your prayers. The message you brought to us, to learn to have love, compassion, and understanding of each other is a hard thing for us to understand, but it makes sense. The Creator does not want us dead, but alive so we may be able to love, respect, and worship him. It is a very strange way for me to see things, after so many seasons of fighting with everyone that is not our relations. Though we Mayas are a peaceful people, our neighbors are always at war with everyone, including us, so we must defend ourselves. I only pray that our enemies do not believe that we have gone mad.

"Do not worry my good friend for I will be taking them all the same message. You see, I am not traveling alone, God is always at my side," I reassured him.

133

"I pray they will listen and embrace you as we have. Now I have something else to talk about with you. Do you remember the night you arrived here?" He asked me. "The Mexica men that were captured that were going to be sacrificed that same night. The Grand Chief spared their lives to see what would happen with you. He wanted to see if the message you brought was one worth listening to. He has let them live, while waiting for you to say what will happen to them."

I was speechless for a moment and realized this was a test by not only the Grand Chief, but by the Creator. They were putting those men's lives in my hands to see if I knew what to do with them. Thoughts raced through my head. What was the answer they were looking for? What do I say to the Grand Chief and the High Priest, I thought to myself. I must not act as though I do not know what to say. I must be decisive and answer with confidence.

"You must give them their freedom," I said, almost without hesitation. "They have the right to live under the laws of God."

He nodded his head as though agreeing with me but did not answer. He moved on to other things that were on his mind. He was full of questions. He wanted to know everything that had happened.

I told him everything; even about the man in the mist who visited me. All the lessons he brought to me and I told him how I was properly put in my place. I did not leave out any details.

I saw a look of anguish or perhaps a small cloud of fear pass over his face. He quickly covered it by looking away from me. He nodded his head in understanding and said he heard of things like that happening to some people. "Yes, I suppose it could be frightening," he said thoughtfully.

"Only if that person knows he is doing wrong or continues doing the same thing after he has been told," I replied. "All the things that were brought and given to me, I have given away to others. I keep only what I need to live comfortably and will have things to give to others as I travel." I reached into my robe and found a large, heavy man's gold ring. "Like this," I showed him. It was the head of a strong looking warrior with long feathers on his headpiece. The feathers curved around the finger, touching on the bottom, completing the ring. His eyes glowed with happiness or was it greed, I thought to myself.

He looked at me in a thoughtful way and told me he also had gifts for me. Asking me to follow him, we retreated into his chambers at the side of the Great Pyramid. He told me this was where he lived and did his praying for guidance. The room he took me to was dimly lit, the air was heavy with smoldering Copal. It was burning in a small clay urn held up by three small odd-looking figurines.

From behind a small table, covered with a dark red cloth, he pulled out a small, beautiful and finely made wooden chest. I noticed the corners; the hinges and the clasp of the chest were made of the same yellow metal that all the jewelry was made of. It must have been a very valuable chest.

He attempted to pick it up, to place it on a bench against the wall beside it, and could not. I asked if I could help him and he stepped aside. I picked it up, but with difficulty. It was very heavy. Opening it, he first reached into it then stopped, turned and looked at me and asked me to pick my own gift.

Shaking my head I said, "No, I can not do that for I do not need anything and if I pick it, it will no longer be a gift from you. It would be something I liked and it would do me no good."

Smiling he agreed with me. "I will find something befitting a person such as you," He said. Reaching in to the chest he pulled out a long heavy chain made of the yellow metal. He put it around my neck. Then he reached in with both hands and came out holding many pieces of beautiful jewelry. There were rings, necklaces, and bracelets. He gave me two handfuls of jewelry to me. I thought he wanted me to select an item as my gift. I put everything on the bench. I was looking at the jewels shaking my head again. "I do not know what to do," I said, to him, "You have already given me this chain, that is enough."

He said, "My son, these gifts, are not for you. They are so you will have many gifts for the people you will meet as you travel. You must take them for I have much more than I will ever need. You have shown me it is not what a person has but how it is used. I will begin to do the same."

It was odd, for I could not recall ever having said anything to him about sharing good fortune with others. It was as the Spirit had said the things I say and do will make a difference.

"In that case, I accept," I said to him, "They are very generous gifts and will go to the people that need them. I put all the jewels in the place I had inside my robe. It was so heavy it kept pulling my robe down so I had to keep pulling it back. Now I knew what my visiting Spirit meant about material possessions becoming a burden to the person that let greed control their feelings.

I also told him somewhere in my past I heard when you had many possessions, if you shared, then more of what you gave away will rush in to fill the space occupied by what you gave away. I do not remember where I heard that, but I believe the Creator looks with favor to those that have a kind and generous heart.

Following him outside again, he led me to a table and two chairs under a large cloth shade. The sun had now climbed to the top of Grandfather Sky and was beginning to get warm.

"I have more gifts for you," he said.

Several priests stood on the side of the Pyramid. They were his helpers and beginners. I noticed Tuleco was nowhere in sight.

He called to them to bring what he had for Kokopelli. They all moved closer to us. Two of them had plates full of food and corn tortillas and of course, chili peppers. We ate and drank with relish, for the little fruit I had eaten with the Grand Chief's wife had not gone very far. We ate without talking. I concentrated on my food and although I was getting used to the hot chilies, I still tried to avoid some of the ones I knew were hotter than others were. I kept my head down and my eyes on what I put in my mouth.

When we were almost finished eating I saw Media Luna signal his men. They reacted as though they had been waiting for just that. Two of them picked up two large woven bags. They stood as high as their waists and carried them to where we were sitting.

Stopping in front of us, they put the bags down. I turned and looked at Media Luna with a question on my face.

"I know you like and will need much of this, so I had my men pack some to take with you on your travels."

"What is it?" I asked him.

"Have you not guessed what it is in the bolsa's (bags)?" He asked.

"No, I have no concept of what it may be," I replied.

"I am giving you enough Copal to last you for many seasons. Since I am talking about seasons, I beg that you not be too hasty in your travels north, for the cold north winds will be starting to find their way south soon. It can be very uncomfortable, the farther north you travel."

I was still looking at the two large bags of Copal. I knew it was highly prized, expensive, and difficult to find. The High Priest was giving me a fortune in Copal.

"Media Luna, how can I carry the bags of Copal, my personal belongings and play my flute all together?" I asked.

"You are planning to go north and up the mountains are you not?" He asked. Then, not giving me an opportunity to answer, "If you go in that direction you will find yourself traveling through the middle of Azteca country. They have many warriors always looking for strangers and people to take prisoner, for their sacrifices. If you go to the large city on top of the mountain, you will find the Mexica people. They are a beautiful, fair, and proud people. Their warriors are very fierce and they are not afraid to fight or die for the leaders and their people. To answer your question about how you will carry all your things. . ."

138

He gave another hand signal and I saw from behind the pyramid, two of his priests escorted the three Mexica prisoners. Their hands tied behind their backs and ankles also tied on short ropes, they were having difficulty moving. They brought them to stand before us.

"Are they to help me carry all that I take with me?" I asked Media Luna.

"Yes, they are yours to use as you see fit, but I would keep them tied up until you know if you can trust them."

The men all had their heads downcast and did not look as though they had been treated very well. They did not look mistreated, just neglected. They probably were not fed too well or very often.

I was up, walked around the table, and stood in front of them. As I stopped, each one lifted their gaze to look at me. Their faces showed no fear or anger. They had a look of resignation as though they had given up hope and were ready for whatever fate brought to them.

As I looked into their eyes, I spoke to them slowly and softly. Their eyes lit up when I spoke their language and seemed to understand them. They immediately started talking to each other. There was a tentative smile here and there.

I called to have the ropes cut and removed from them. I told them they were to help and guide me. That I had asked for their freedom and it was granted.

As soon as the ropes were removed, the priests moved back, a little afraid of the warriors who were now free. The prisoners stood there uncertain as to what to do. I saw there was still much food on the table, I motioned them to move closer and told them to eat their fill. They stood still not knowing if they could trust us, so I asked them to tell me what to eat. They looked at each other and all pointed to one of the dishes. I dipped a spoon and stirred it then took a large spoonful of it and ate it. That proved to them the food was not poisoned. They stepped up close to the table and ate like starved men.

Media Luna came close to me and asked me when and how I had learned how to speak Mexica, and for that matter to speak the Mayan language.

"You must believe me when I tell you that I did not even realize I was speaking a different language until you pointed it out to me," I answered him.

Then Media Luna slapped his forehead with the palm of his hand and exclaimed how stupid he felt knowing who and what I was, to think there was anything I would not know. "You have to forgive me, for I see you do so many things just like we do and hearing about your exploits, I forget and think of you as human."

I did not answer him for I also wondered how I knew all that came to me.

As the men finished eating, they came and sat down at my feet, to show they accepted me for the moment and to wait for me to tell them what they were to do next.

Getting anxious to leave, I stood up, put my old robe over my shoulders, and told them to pick up the rest of the things I would be taking with me. They complied with my orders and after they were ready to go I turned to Media Luna and thanked him for all he had done for me and the gifts he had given me. I told him that I was taking his medicine with me and spread it wherever I travel.

He wished me well and to go with God, that he would be praying for my safe travels. He also told me how to get on the best trail to head north and sent two of his priests to escort us to the outer limits of the village. He said that it was best because the people of the village would recognize the men as Mexica warriors and might cause trouble.

CHAPTER 15

THE JOURNEY NORTH

I started walking and the men followed me. Each carrying some of the things I would need. We moved quickly for I wanted to be as far away from the city as we could get before we had to stop and make camp for the night. It took the rest of the sun before we were well clear of all the dwellings and before Grandfather Sun went to sleep in the West. I was anxious to be away from the people of the large city. They had been looking at us oddly because they recognized us as strangers and I did not want them to be alarmed. The presence of the two holy men prevented them from doing anything about us leaving.

As we reached the last houses, the two priests waved their farewells and turned back. They disappeared quickly into the gathering darkness.

I spotted a faint trail that ran a little west from the one we were on and took it. I explained that we did not want to camp too close to the trail. They wholeheartedly agreed for they were in fact still in enemy territory and danger.

We found a secluded place under a large old tree. I told them we would sleep without a fire and leave early at sunrise, the following morning. One by one, they gathered leaves from one of the bushes and rubbed them all over their bodies. One of them saw me looking at them and said that it was to keep off the insects. They all lay down, bunched up the same leaves and used them for headrests. The weather was still hot and we needed nothing else.

Next morning well before sunrise, I rose and went to a large bush to relieve myself. Being light sleepers they all rose quietly and answered the call of nature. We all gathered around the packs and I took out a pile of corn tortillas and handed each man two of them. From another woven bag, I pulled out some pieces of dried deer meat. With a knife, I did not know he had, one of the men offered to cut it. I nodded my head and he did.

As we stood there in the morning mist, eating cold venison and tortillas, I asked them their names.

The one with the knife said he was called Aguila (Eagle); he seemed to be the spokesman for them and a leader. He was as tall as I was and very muscular. He had a golden bronze color and several scars on his chest, arms, and legs.

The next one said he was called El Lobo (The Wolf). He was not as tall or as built as Aguila but still a warrior. The last one was the timid one; named Dos Piedras (Two Stones).

Then Aguila asked me who I was and why the High Priest treated me as he did. He asked where I learned to speak Mexica. He was full of questions. Lobo told him not to ask so many questions of the man that saved their lives. Aguila ignored him when I said I did not mind answering his questions.

"First," I told them, "I am called Kokopelli. The reason the Priests treated me the way they did was because. . ."

Before I could finish what I was saying, Dos Piedras interrupted and said he heard the minor priests say I was a God. They had not heard of me because locked away they had talked to no one. They looked at me with different eyes. Aguila was more respectful but not intimidated.

"As far as being able to speak your language, it seems I can understand anyone I speak with. I believe it is a gift from God that I can do these things," I told them.

"Does your God protect you?" challenged Aguila, holding the knife with the cutting edge up.

"I do not know," I replied, "I have never had to go through that test yet."

"I for one, do not believe we owe you anything for saving our lives," he said, "And you are my enemy."

"Why am I your enemy?" I asked, "Have I ever shown that I do not trust or value you as a human being. I took the chance that you would at least try to understand what I was trying to do because you seem to be intelligent enough to see."

El Lobo tried to calm him down by saying, "Aguila, what are you doing? He is the one that got us our freedom, leave him alone."

143

Angrily, he moved toward me still not sure what to make of me. He said, "If you are a God then I can cut you, and you will not bleed." He jumped forward with his knife raised to slash me.

A large tree root that had not been there before appeared and tripped him. He went headfirst into the base of the tree and knocked himself unconscious. Almost immediately, a large bump appeared on his forehead and he started bleeding. The other two stood transfixed with surprise at what Aguila was doing.

I went to him, knelt down, and asked for the gourd with water. I wet his face and put a little water into his mouth. He coughed and awakened from his senselessness to find me giving him the water.

He rose to his feet angrily and said, "I am not done with you yet." He was holding the knife low by his right. He swung his arm to the rear. Bringing the knife close to his leg, he was going to stab me. I happened to be standing to his left and he had to bring the knife from behind his right leg and stab toward the left. Somehow, he brought the knife too close to his leg because, instead of stabbing me he stuck the knife into the side of his own leg.

The cut was not bad, but enough to make him stop to think of what he was trying to do to me. He stood looking at me in visible pain and finally dropped the knife and his gaze. He quietly said that he had wanted to know if my God protected me and found out he did. He also said that it was not that he was clumsy for he was a good warrior. It was not like him to trip and fall or stab his own leg. It had to be God's intervention on my behalf.

144

He apologized and swore he would never question me again, if I would forgive him. I did and it was over. The others would follow me and do as I asked. What puzzled them the most was that I never tried to run or get away from his threat and the knife. I stood and faced a good warrior without fear, done nothing and defeated him. I could hear them talking about it later.

I told him to pick up the knife that we might have need of it later. He picked it up and he hid it somewhere in his loincloth.

We moved out and back to the main trail. Traveling was slow because there was fog lying close to the ground. The trail was quiet and it cast an eerie feeling on us. It was still difficult to see. The birds and insects had not started moving and making their noises yet.

We were all a bit leery traveling on a well-used trail for we could never know who or what we might run into. We walked quietly and silently, listening for any sound not made by us.

About midmorning, we came to a fork in the trail and stopped to one side to rest and have a drink of water. I asked them if they knew of the trail ahead.

"I have been on this trail before," said Aguila, "And if I remember correctly, if we stay on it, we will eventually get to the village of Tipu. From there, we could find other trails to lead us to our home, the land of the Azteca and the Mexica. If we take the right fork, it will take us to the village of Palenque. It is the shorter of the two trails and I am more familiar with it."

"What will we be facing on this trail?" I asked him.

"We would have to cross one river before Palenque and then a small range of hills and mountains. In amongst the hills we will find Palenque."

"How many suns do you feel it will take us?" I asked him.

"It should not be more than as many fingers I have on both my hands," he replied holding his hands up.

"We will take the right fork then," I said as I got to my feet and started walking. I turned to Aguila and asked if he wanted to take the lead since he was more familiar with the trail.

I saw him smile and nod his head saying that he was happy to have this honor. He set a ground eating pace, but it was not so fast that anyone had to struggle to keep up.

When we continued on our journey the fog had cleared. We met and passed a few people on the trail. They moved quickly and quietly by us as though they feared us.

I did not want to play my flute for fear of attracting bandits or other bad elements to us. We were not armed well enough to defend ourselves. We moved on quietly and as fast as possible trying to cover as much distance as we could. No one complained nor asked to stop. We could still be in danger.

The second night we stopped late and built a small fire. We roasted some dried deer meat, warmed the tortillas, and made a small pot of café. It turned out hot and strong.

We all shared the food and drink equally. It was not something they were used to and wanted to wait for me to eat and drink first. I did take the first drink and bite of food, but then I passed it to them. They drank slowly as though waiting for me to say something to them. When I did not they relaxed and enjoyed the tortillas, meat, and coffee.

The next few suns were a succession of almost identical suns. The only difference was when we would stop at night one or two of them would go off into the jungle and try to find food. More often than not, they would return with at least some kind of fruit. A couple of occasions Aguila brought back birds of some kind. I do not know what they were but they tasted very good roasted over the flames.

On the eighth sun, we came out of the trees to the bank of a river. Before us was a wide but shallow river. We walked across it with the water never going much past our waists. On the other side, we found a good shade under a small tree and stopped to rest. I wanted and took the opportunity to wash myself in the river. As I splashed in the water, Dos Piedras and El Lobo also got into the water.

"Why is Aguila not getting into the water?" I asked.

"He will later, after one of us is out. Someone has to keep watch to make sure no one surprises us," answered Dos Piedras.

After we bathed and rested, we ate and bedded down for the night. Sleeping in an open area, and out from the jungle canopy, we enjoyed seeing Grandfather Sun awaken. As the sun rose, I heard the many birds begin their chattering, and morning songs. Next morning we continued on the trail to Palenque. I noticed their step seemed to pick up and we moved faster.

"Now that we are away from so many people," said Aguila, "Will you play your flute for us?" Dos Piedras said he heard me play and it sounded beautiful.

"I would be happy to play it for you," I replied. I put the flute to my lips and started to play a happy tune in rhythm with our steps.

We walked over a small hill. Spread before us was the city of Palenque, its narrow streets teeming with people. As we walked into the city I heard people saying, "Kokopelli, it is Kokopelli." To show who I was I continued to play my flute.

I could not believe it was possible someone knew about me here when we were so far from Chi-Chen Itza.

Aguila, El Lobo, and Dos Piedras seemed surprised and proud to be walking with me.

Apparently, the priests of Palenque knew of our coming for they were waiting for us. We were escorted to the home of the High Priest of this beautiful and large settlement. He had food and drinks ready for us when we arrived.

I recognized one of the priests there because he had come to the village on the ocean and spent several weeks with us learning about the Temascal and how to pour water.

While sitting down eating, we had an opportunity to talk. I asked him if he had a Temascal going and he quietly answered, "The High Priest, Pantera Negra (Black Panther) did not give me permission to start one."

"Perhaps now I am here I can give you that permission."

Later I did have an opportunity to bring up the subject about the Temascal with Pantera Negra. He acted as though he had always been in favor of having one and said it in front of everyone. He said they must build one as soon as possible. He made it sound as though it was his idea. Perhaps that had been his reluctance, that it was not his idea at the beginning. I think it was also prompted by the gift of gold I gave him.

Things went well in Palenque; we remained there several moons after I was told again about the cold weather in the land of the Aztecs. I did not feel that I wanted to face the cold and walk in the rain and snow. We remained until all those that needed to learn the Ways had received the knowledge I came to share.

The three men became my good companions and helpers. They did not seem anxious to keep going after we settled there. In fact, when we did leave, Dos Piedras met a young woman, married her, and decided to remain in Palenque.

There were some adventures with young women who offered to be of assistance to me. They did help me, with the cooking, bathing, giving me rubdowns and keeping my bed warm. Of all of the women that helped me, none were as good to me as Estrella Blanca. I would feel that ache in my heart, now and again, missing her and thinking of our experiences together. She left a big impression in my heart and mind. In my thoughts, I wished I could have brought her with me.

Early the following season I decided we had been there long enough. I felt I had taught all I could and one of my housekeepers was starting to get too serious about me staying to live there forever. I told her I had many people to meet and many others to help.

She told me that now I was leaving she could tell me something that had been kept from me. She wanted me to know that at least five girls in Palenque would be having my children and I would always be remembered in a good way. She cried when she said it. I never saw her again, not even when we left.

The following morning, with Aguila leading the way we set off well before the town of Palenque awakened to the new sun. We traveled far, not stopping until the sun was getting ready to go to sleep. It became hard to tell one sun from another, as it was mixed in with walking and playing my flute.

The country started to change. We were climbing as we started getting into the mountains, but still the land was covered with jungle. It was a beautiful land. We brought an abundance of fruit and dried meat. Being healthy and strong, we did not need very much. We would come upon small villages and replenish our supplies. Usually, all I had to do is play my flute and people would know of me and give us what we needed. I was glad that I still had one and a half sacks of the Copal, though I had given a lot away and used it for many ceremonies.

Often, we were invited to spend the night in their homes. The village elders would have beautiful gifts for me. I would always give them something in return.

They would offer their daughters to me. Somehow, the word spread that I was a God and it was a privilege for a girl to conceive a child with me. I do not know who or why someone started that story about me, but it was impossible for me to reach a village that did not offer me many things like that. It could be embarrassing.

We crossed a large river at a crossing where a man had a large canoe. He took us across to a small village that lay on the other side. Again, I was received with respect because I was Kokopelli. They knew of me and wanted to hear what was going on in other villages.

After we had eaten that evening, almost all the people of the village gathered around the main village fire to listen to me talk. I told them about what I had learned at Chi-Chen Itza. What we had done on the coast, learning to pray in the Temascal and how I taught others to do the ceremonies. I also played my flute for them until I was tired and stopped.

It was an enjoyable evening. As the gathering began to break up, three of the elders called me to the side to talk. They asked if I would remain at their village to teach them the Ways. I agreed to stay at least one moon. I thought by then they should learn enough to be able to help themselves.

They offered me their home. That night as I was getting ready to sleep, I heard the curtain at the front entrance open. There appeared a little girl of about ten summers. She was small, thin and seemed to be very sad. She had long hair, a beautiful little face, with large, brown eyes.

I asked her what I could do for her.

She was looking down at her feet as though embarrassed. She said quietly that she did not know what she was supposed to do. She had only been told that she was to sleep with me.

I could not believe what I was hearing. I stood there thinking for a few moments, not saying anything. My anger at what they had done slowly started rising. I felt insulted that they would think that I, Kokopelli would stoop to that level of violating a child such as that small virginal little girl child. It made me angrier than I had ever been in my

151

life. Still having my robe on, I took her by her thin little arm and walked her back to her parent's home.

I did not bother to announce myself. I walked straight into their house to find the father and his wife both sitting on the side of their bed. They both seemed to be sad and the mother was crying softly.

I asked them what was the meaning of them sending this small child to me to use. Why had they even thought that I would do such a thing as abuse an innocent little girl like her? I told them that I felt insulted by what they had done.

They said the only reason they had offered their daughter, was they wanted to have a grandchild from me. All their other girls were older and had families of their own. The father also said that she was the only thing of value and the very best they had to offer me. Crying, the mother said they did not want to do this but thought I might be insulted if I was offered an older or wiser girl. The mother continued that it had broken her heart but she was offering her daughter to me as a token of appreciation for me staying to teach them the Spiritual Ways.

"This is not the way to start being Spiritual," I said. "It crosses my mind to just move on the next sun. This insult is so great that I must think of what I will do about it. If any person ever stooped to something as low as this, God himself would find him and make him suffer more than anyone has ever suffered. Just the thought of using this child in this way, turns my stomach," Disgusted, I turned and walked out.

Going back to the house where I was staying, my mind was full of thoughts of what had just happened. I heard that if a girl conceived a child with me her family never had to

152

worry about anything ever again. I understood the desperation that poor people felt and to what lengths they were forced to go in their desperation. I also thought that had been the only reason they offered what they had. The sad part about it was I did not believe a child that small could even conceive.

As I lay there, I prayed for guidance as to what I should do about this. Should I stay and teach them as I was supposed to do or should I feel so offended that I must move on and leave them in their misery. I lay very still and waited for my answer. I believe my tired body was finally relaxing and I started to fall asleep. Suddenly I felt a presence in the room with me. It was my old friend, the Spirit from the beach, from so long ago. I sat up and greeted him saying it was good to see him again.

He smiled and said I had passed another test. This situation was placed before me to see how and if I respected the laws of the Creator and I had done well. "The Creator is happy with the way you think and act. It is one thing to have a woman that understands what is going to happen and quite another to force oneself on to an innocent child. We commend you on your behavior and ethics."

"I am still hurt that they would think I would even do such a thing," I exclaimed.

"Think of their situation. They did not truly want to offer that child. Why do you think her mother was crying?" He asked. "Just the thought of her little girl being violated was breaking her heart. You made her very happy by bringing her back intact. As for your feelings being hurt, think of the grief they went through just agreeing to do this. Think of what would make them happy. The reason they offered their daughter was to convince you to stay and teach them the Ways of the Temascal. You must grant them that. Also a little bit of wealth would go a long way to help them have a better life and that is all they want. You still have many things of value to give. Gift them something to make their lives easier. Forget how you feel and do what you have chosen to do, teach them and help them find the Ways."

As suddenly as he appeared, he was gone. My prayers answered my mind now at peace with relief I laid down and was soon asleep.

The next sun I let them know I decided to stay and teach them the Ways. Since Aguila and Lobo already helped me in the past, they were a great deal of help. They did not know how to build a Temascal out of brush, so they also had to learn. I explained it normally was built of dirt bricks (adobe) and mud, but since we did not have any we would build it out of saplings and brush.

We gathered all the things we needed and had our first Temascal ceremony. For the next moon, we had Sweat Lodge ceremonies almost everyday. One of the elders, Bravo (Brave One) was always by me ready and willing to learn. He received that name because in battle he would always be the one in front. It seemed that every place I went to teach the Temascal, someone would stand out to pass on the teachings and Ways to others. Bravo was the one in this village.

After seven suns, I asked him to lead the lodge, to pour water for us. I wanted him to start getting experience. He learned quickly, so after we had our one lodge, if we had some men that did not get in, I would let him run the second lodge for them. There never seemed to be enough space in the Temascal for everyone that wanted to come in.

At the end of the short period of teaching them I told him that he was ready to be the leader for them. I also told him that he must find a younger man to teach as a helper.

The morning we were ready to leave everyone in the village was there to see us off. I called the little girl that had been offered to me and both her parents. Out of the folds of my robe, I pulled out a short but heavy gold chain and talked to them.

I said, "I wanted them to know the little girl was more valuable than gold because she was their future. She was the one that was going to make them live forever. She was going to carry their blood into the future. As long as she lives and gives you grandchildren your blood will never die. You must never offer her to anyone ever again until she is ready and old enough to choose her own husband. She is more valuable than you think for she has brought you this." I put the chain around her little neck.

Looking at her father and mother I said, "This is very valuable. It will bring you many of the things you need and want. Each link has a lot of value. As you need it, cut off one link and trade for what you need. One will get you goats and chickens; another link will get you seeds and a place to plant them. However, never show anyone that you have this gift, as there are those that will attempt to take it from you. After you get prosperous, you must share with the rest of your families. Will you remember everything I have said to you?"

They both had tears in their eyes as they nodded to me, unable to speak.

I turned and walked away, knowing that if they did as I suggested, they would do well. If they did not then I could do no more to help them. They would at least have had an opportunity.

CHAPTER 16

MOVING WEST

For several moons Aguila, Lobo and I traveled spreading the word of the Temascal, love, and compassion. We walked and saw many different people and cultures. Some accepted what we had to teach and others were openly hostile toward us. I did not feel I had enough life to attempt to teach the Ways to everyone we encountered or talked to. This path was for those that wanted it and it was not for everyone.

Instead of going toward Mexica country we walked toward the West where I was told was another ocean. I was curious to see it. What was so interesting was that at most places they had heard of me and that I had information and stories from many places.

I received many gifts and gave most of them away in other villages. I was always given the best gifts, so when I gave them away, I was giving the best to others. Soon my name Kokopelli was related to wonderful gifts. It was a good way to be known.

After many moons of traveling, one evening we arrived on the coast. It was called Clhuatlan, located right on the shore of a beautiful calm ocean. It too, was surrounded by thick vegetation, different kinds of wild life, and colored birds. Although it was also thick jungle growth with an ocean close by, it felt different from the place where I first arrived.

There again I taught and showed the people the Temascal ceremony. There were only a few interested because it was a hard way to follow. Many people, I was teaching the ceremony, would come once and few came back for more. I always thought only the ones that were supposed to be there would come. I always told people this was not for the faint of heart. The Temascal was hard, but the rewards were great.

I could not recall how long we stayed there but it was perhaps two moons. One morning I told my now close friends, Aguila and El Lobo, that it was a good sun to travel. We would be leaving and moving on to the north. I told them I wanted to stay close to the shore because I felt comfortable traveling within sight of it. It brought peace into my life and tranquility to my sleep.

They responded that they would stay with me for another moon and then they would be close to a good trail that would lead them back to their own country.

We left and walked for many suns. We crossed many creeks and rivers leading to and emptying themselves into the ocean. The sun arrived that we found the trail that led to Teotihuacan. .

I knew the moment had arrived to say farewell to my friends. We were all quiet for a long moment. I embraced each of them and before I let them go I gave them the last two heavy gold armbands. These were still from the two hands full of jewelry Media Luna had given me. I thanked them for all they had done for me and for being such good companions. I told them to always be well. They reassured me they would, for I had taught them the Ways of the Temascal well and in my honor, they would erect one in their city and continue to teach it to others.

I started walking north again. They stood as if undecided as to what to do and looking as though they were lost little boys. It made my heart break to be losing two good friends, but I had to travel alone from now on. I consoled myself by thinking at least I had their friendship for many, many moons.

They called after me, if I was sure I wanted to travel on alone or come with them. That I would be treated better than I had been treated anywhere we had been to.

I thanked them again and said my mind was made up and I had to follow my destiny.

I traveled for many seasons. I walked as though the wind was my guide. For some reason I would travel north for a few suns and for no reason at all I would change direction and travel west the following sun. I met many people and taught about love, compassion, and the Temascal. I told stories of my travels and taught other things, for I had gained knowledge from the many people I met on my journey.

Once I traveled south to find Teotihuacan to see my good friends and visit with them. When I arrived, it was in the middle of the cold weather and I had a difficult few suns in the city. There were too many people and everyone was either in a hurry or too busy to talk to me. I could never find my two friends. I left going to the lower country and the coast where it was always warm.

The seasons came and went and I just kept walking and playing my flute.

Although I was treated very well everywhere I went and had the company of many women, I was still a lonely man. I accepted my life the way it was, to spread love, compassion and to teach about the Sacred Ways.

CHAPTER 17

WAKING UP

I woke up and I am still lying off the side of the trail I had fallen off. I can barely feel my feet, so there is not much back pain, but I still cannot move. I am cold, so very cold. I listen to see if I can hear anyone on the trail above me. I hear nothing, no noise, or sounds at all. The constant wind was my only companion. It talks to me when it blows through the short sagebrush.

The sky I notice is dark and heavy with clouds. Are they rain or snow clouds? I wonder. At this height it could be either one of the two, I think. I pray it does not snow until someone finds me. Deep inside I feel it is snow, because if it were not, it would not be as cold as it is.

I remember my dream. It is still very vivid in my mind. I am surprised that even in my dream I can remember so much of my life. I guess I am recalling only the good things that happened in my travels. Thinking of my dream helps me forget my chest pain. I lay there and wonder what happened to the people I have met through the seasons. I think of Aguila and El Lobo, and wonder if they still follow the Ways. I miss my friends and when I think of them, I still get a lump in my throat. I guess we were closer than I realized when we were traveling together. How I miss their company.

When the blowing wind touches the middle of my body, it feels cold. I move my hand down to cover myself, thinking my robe has fallen off. I touch myself where I am cold and find out that I have urinated on myself. The urine, feels as though it is starting to freeze, it is very cold. Out of curiosity, I touch my behind and am surprised to find I have also defecated in my breechcloth. I feel shame and disgust at myself for I have never done that. I think of what people will think when they find me. I must have done it when I was asleep. I am so ashamed of what I have done.

Well until I am found, there is nothing I can do about it. I tell myself to relax and be patient, someone will surely come soon. I lay there because I can do nothing else and my mind starts drifting again.

I feel so alone and sorry for myself. I am sad about the situation in which I find myself. I feel tears form in my eyes and brush them away. By not staying at the last village where I could be warm and fed, one careless step has brought me here to this. At least I can move my arms, I think to myself. Then I force myself to relax and enjoy the solitude. As I lay there, I try to make friends with the cold, my chest pain, and the wind.

Little by little, my body begins to relax and I seem to be warmer. I wait and listen. The wind seems to be easing a little. I feel myself getting sleepy again. I look at the sky and it does not look as cloudy or as unfriendly. My eyes close and open again briefly, then close. I drift deeper and deeper, until I find myself back in my dream.

CHAPTER 18

DREAMING AGAIN

When I left Teotihuacan, I walked north and west. I stayed on trails I could find and I found myself in a great desert. The only place to find water was in the few villages I found two or three suns away from each other.

When I had traveled north for many suns, I found a village. These people would hunt deer by running after it until the deer fell from exhaustion. That was their way of hunting without the need for bows and arrows or lances. They called themselves the Tarahumara.

161

On another occasion I traveled into the mountains of the north central part of Aztec lands. High up in the mountains I found a people who were fierce, loyal and tough. They loved a good fight and did not mind going out of their way to find it. They were also fair and kind to those they liked or respected. I attempted to teach them the Ways of the Sweat Lodge but they refused to listen to me. They were very loyal to their own beliefs and did not care to learn anything else. I spent several suns there, told some of my stories, and taught a few of the younger boys how to make and play the flute.

I left again, traveling north. For many suns I traveled, until I found myself on another ocean, but this ocean was made of growing grass. It was so large that I could not see far enough to see where it ended. I moved on it for many suns, looking for a village or people, and all I found was more grass and the ceaseless wind.

One evening, tired from walking and the monotony of this great grass ocean, I found a large old tree and decided to stop early to make camp and rest. After I had eaten, not having anything to see except waving grass, I sat down to play my flute to the heavens. I wanted to send music to the Creator so He would help me find my way through this endless sea of grass. The sounds that came from my flute were lonely and sad. I guess I was reflecting on the way I felt.

I gathered all the dead branches I could find to build a fire. When Grandfather sun was settling into the western horizon, I started a small fire. I kept it small because wood was hard to find and there was very little of it. I did find old droppings from a large animal and found that they burnt well, though the smoke had an unusual smell to it.

I sat with the small fire as a companion as I played my flute trying to lift my spirits. I sat up for a long while until Grandmother Moon looked at me from the eastern edge of Mother Earth. Now I felt like sleeping and resting. As I lay waiting for sleep to arrive, I talked to the stars. I asked them to guide my way to other people for I missed the company.

I slept, but was uneasy in my sleep. I felt something was coming that I did not understand and it made me uncomfortable.

It was late. Something woke me. I looked at Grandmother Moon and she was more than half way across the sky. What had awakened me? I asked myself. I lay very quietly listening to the night noises. At first, all I could hear were the crickets chirping. Suddenly, even they stopped talking. In the distance I could hear a rumbling sound, one I had never heard before. Then I heard many sounds of grunting and snorting. I did not know what it was, so I stood up and faced where the sounds were coming from, the south. The slight breeze was coming from the south and I could smell animal hair and sweat. In the moonlight, the grassy ocean was moving. Dust was rising above whatever was coming. Looking out at the sight, I realized they had already surrounded the tree nearby.

Alarmed, I climbed into the tree as high as I could go, and waited. Soon I recognized that it was a huge herd of bison. There had to be as many as the stars in the sky. They had surrounded my tree and kept walking past it.

Suddenly they stopped moving and started bedding down. I supposed they were tired and needed to rest. I was stuck on my perch high above them.

At sunup, they all begin to rise and browse, but moving north as they ate. The animals kept coming and coming. There seemed to be no end to the herd. I was still sitting on top of the tree waiting for them to leave.

I was in the tree for three suns waiting and watching. I had never seen such an event as this. I was grateful that I had the opportunity, but wished I could have walked away whenever I chose to do so. As it was, I had to wait for them to get by me and let me down.

As soon as I touched the ground, I heard someone yell. Several young warriors came running and stopped all around me. They were speaking a language very different from any of the others I heard in all my travels. I could still understand what they were saying. I greeted them and told them I had been stuck up in the tree for three suns waiting for the animals to go by. They burst out laughing, thinking of me being perched up on a branch that long.

Laughing, one of them asked me what I did when I had to follow Mother Nature's call.

When I told him that I just sat on a branch and answered Mother Nature, they all laughed so hard, some were rolling on the ground.

About then the elders walked up and looked me over. One asked me where I was from and what I was doing here. I told them I was just a traveler caught up in the middle of all the animals. He wanted to know where I learned to speak their tongue. I replied that it was a gift from the

Great Spirit. They stood for a moment then walked off. One of them turned and waved at me to follow them.

There were many people with them, men, women, and children. We walked for a far distance, keeping just behind the large herd of bison.

They were dragging long poles with Bison hides on them. When we stopped, I was amazed at how quickly the women put up their round shelters. They used the poles as the frame and then covered them with the hides. It made a small but comfortable home out of the elements.

When camp was made that night, I talked to them about my travels. They cooked fresh bison meat roasted over a fire. It was delicious, after being on a steady diet of dried meat and berries for so long. After we had all eaten, I played my flute for them. When I finished playing, they put up a large drum and started drumming and singing. It was beautiful the way they sang. Then all the people started dancing in a circle. We talked and they danced until it was almost dawn. I had talked about the Temascal and why people would do this ceremony. They were very interested and wanted to know all about it.

I stayed with them until they reached their winter camp. They had hunted the bison all summer and put up dried meat for the many winter moons. Each night I would tell them more about the Temascal and answer their questions. Several of the young men were very interested in the flute, so I taught them how to make and play it.

I taught them about the Temascal and they were so interested that I showed them how to build it. We made it out of the most common vegetation around; they were long tall saplings (willow). We had many ceremonies so they could learn how to do them. They loved it because they could take their Spirituality with them and build new lodges, wherever they found themselves.

One morning as I was coming out of my tipi I heard a big commotion coming from one of the tipis. Looking in that direction, I saw two women holding a younger woman's arms, attempting to restrain her. I went to them and asked what was the matter. They told me that she had something wrong with her head. Her husband could not control her and her children were afraid of her.

They also said that she had been like that when things got bad. It really got worse after she gave birth to her last child, who was now six moons old. She would talk to herself, mumbling things. They told me that she would have visions of spirits telling her things. The young woman was very upset and the other two women did not know what to do. They asked me if I could help her. I knew the Temascal would help. We had used it before to heal so many others.

We prepared stones and built the fire. Before the stones were hot, she calmed down and was more pleasant. They told her I was going to help her.

When we were ready to go into the lodge, the two women asked if they could be inside with her. I told them I needed and wanted them in the lodge.

The prayers in the lodge were very intense and sincere. I had twenty stones brought in and it was hot. The woman went through a life changing experience that day. It was as though the heat and prayers had purged whatever was bothering her troubled mind. She prayed very hard to have her prayers answered. Before the lodge was complete, she apologized to her mother and older sister for all the things she said and did.

As we left the lodge, it seemed the whole village had gathered around. They heard everything and were surprised at the change in her. She was very peaceful and calm now.

One of the elders said that this proved how powerful the ceremony was. They were going to make it a part of their lives from then on.

I remained with them teaching as much as I could. Then one morning when I emerged from my tipi, there was frost on everything. I told them I must head south, for I did not like the cold and snow.

They made me a mixture of berries, mint leaves, wild onions and dried, ground up, bison meat and bison fat. They called it Pemmican. It was delicious, nourishing and could sustain a person on the trail for a long while.

The very next morning, I set out early heading south, after I bid everyone farewell.

I traveled south and west. The land I traveled started rising. Even though I was going south, it was not getting any warmer. I seemed to be climbing higher and higher. I reached a place so high the snow was lying thick on the ground. I climbed even higher, until I reached the western edge of a mountain.

Grandfather Sun was getting low in the western horizon, so I decided to camp until morning. I had to build a small fire to ward off the cold. The Plains people had given me a large tanned elk hide to bring for the cold. Together with my robe, that kept the wind off me, but did little to keep out the cold. I ate a piece of bison meat and a small helping of the pemmican.

I slept, but not well. When the wood burned down, the cold, like an enemy would strike at me without mercy. I had to stay awake most of the night just to feed wood to the fire to stay warm. At least, I thought to myself, it is not snowing. As I sat by the fire, all I could think of was the warm places where I had been in the south by the ocean and the jungles. They seemed so far away now and they were another world.

Morning arrived slowly. I had to wait for Grandfather Sun to light my way down the western face of the mountain. I walked down carefully. The trail I found was a narrow game trail. There was a layer of ice all over everything on the trail and my moccasins were wet and slippery. I had to walk with great care to keep from falling.

When I reached the bottom, it was a great relief and I was exhausted. It had taken me the entire sun. I found a spot between two large boulders that offered me shelter. After I built a fire, the large stones reflected heat and made me very comfortable. This was the driest and warmest I had been since I left my friends on the plains. I camped there recuperating for two suns before I continued west.

I traveled west for five suns. Until one morning as I was walking, I saw fresh small footprints in the snow. The snows were getting deep and it was starting to snow again when I found the faint trail. Moving quickly, I followed them. I did not want to lose whoever was leaving the tracks. The tracks were following the face of a huge solid rock cliff. I came around a protrusion on the rock and found a tall ladder. I had to stand back to look upwards to see where it went.

From the top of the ladder, I saw a young girl look down at me and she smiled. She waved at me to come up. As I started climbing the ladder, it felt weak and frail, but held strong, until I reached the first level.

I was amazed to see several other levels sitting one on top of the other. The whole village was located under a huge overhang of solid rock. There were ladders going to each level.

I heard a noise behind me and turned to look. There were several men standing there. They greeted me, each of them smiling. As we started talking one of them pulled the ladder up and laid it on the roof. When I looked at him with a question on my face, he said, that kept anyone they did not want, from climbing up.

Once again, I had to go through my stories of where I came from, who I was, and where I was going. This gift of being able to understand everyone I talked to was a blessing. I told them I was called Kokopelli. I played the flute and brought stories from people far away.

The elder that talked to me the most said they were called The Anasazi. When he spoke their name, he said it with such pride. After we visited a while they invited me to eat with them. We went into the room on that same level, where there was an oven with a good fire going. Some of the women were cooking bread in the oven. It smelled good and my stomach started growling.

They had closed the opening with a large heavy woven blanket. The room had some high openings for light. On the floor were small thick woven rugs for everyone to sit on. They asked me to sit as all the others found places, leaning against the walls. Almost immediately, the girl that had waved to me brought me a clay plate of deer meat, some brown, delicious beans, and a piece of bread, fresh from the oven. With it, she brought me a clay cup of water and a small wooden spoon.

I looked in her eyes as she handed me the food and saw that she was not as young as I thought when I had first seen her. She appeared to be about twenty-three summers old.

I waited until I saw one of them start to eat before I put some food into my mouth. I sat there enjoying the first hot food I had eaten in many suns. I chewed it slowly savoring the wonderful taste. Everyone else was eating and enjoying the evening.

After we finished eating one of the elders spoke to me. He wanted to know where I was going, when the girl, Agua Dulce (Sweet Water) had seen me.

"You know," said one of the younger men, "She left her tracks so you could find them. We all know how to hide our tracks so well that many of our enemies have tried to find us and cannot."

I told the elder I was trying to get south to where it was warm and dry. I could not stay, for my bones were starting to bother me when I got cold. I explained that I spent much of my youth in the south and thought of it often.

"Well for tonight, if you wish, you may spend the night here and let us see what the new sun brings."

"I accept your generous invitation," I replied thankfully. "I am tired and need the rest." Then I asked if they would like me to play my flute for them. They all nodded their heads enthusiastically. I took my flute out and started playing a soft but beautiful song. I could see in their faces that the song was touching their hearts.

170

I looked to where Agua Dulce was sitting and she was mesmerized by the sound of my flute. After I played two songs, I stopped and told them about my travels and the people I encountered. Late that night after one of my stories, I stood and stretched. They all got to their feet and started leaving. The elder that talked the most to me I found out was the village leader. He told me for that night, I could sleep in the room where I was, and he left.

I gathered a few of the rugs left on the floor and made myself a place to sleep. I lay down after I removed my robe and was naked on top of the rugs. I was almost asleep when I heard the blanket to the other room move. The oven still had wood burning in it and it kept the entire room very warm and gave off the only light in the room. I saw someone walk between the oven and me.

When she knelt by me I knew who it was, it was Agua Dulce. She whispered she wanted to visit and see if I needed anything, like covers or water. I told her I was fine and did not need anything. She stood, quietly for a moment, and then sat down next to me on the rugs. She wanted to be with me, I thought. Her mannerisms told me that, but did not know how to start or what to say. I thought I would help her. She could leave if that was not what she wanted.

"There is one thing I need," as I reached up to grab her arm and pull her gently down to me. "I need someone to help me stay warm," I said.

She did not resist as I laid her next to me. I put my hand on her stomach and I could feel her heart beating wildly. I slowly lifted her dress and when it was up to her pubic area, I touched her and found she was not wearing anything under it.

I was not as young as I used to be so it took me a while to get to that point we all search for. However, it was to her advantage, for I took that opportunity to explore her body from one end to the other. She lay quietly enjoying my actions with my hands and fingers. Everything I did, I did it slowly. Through the years, and with some help from Estrella Blanca, I had learned much about how to make women happy and I used it all on Agua Dulce. I also knew that the only attraction to me was that I was a stranger and different from all the men she knew here.

After a long while of stimulating her, she was ready to receive me. I positioned myself over her and asked if she could put me into her opening. She clumsily tried to help me but could not. I went forward to my left elbow and used my right to place myself into the right place. I slowly started pushing and heard her catch her breath. I pushed a little harder and she stifled a cry that wanted out. I pushed again not realizing what was wrong, then something gave and I was in her all the way. She was wiggling as if in pain.

"What is wrong?" I asked her.

"You are the first man for me," she said breathing softly.

The girl had been a virgin. In all my years of being with women, I had never experienced this and was overcome with compassion and love for this girl who had given me her ultimate gift.

I was very gentle with her now, knowing the truth. I stayed with her until she found out that making love was not all pain. She left quietly to return to her own bed before anyone knew she had been gone.

The next morning I got up early thinking someone might be coming to eat or wanted to be in this room. I was right.

172

Shortly after I was up two women walked into the room and added wood to the fire. During the night, I got up and put wood into the oven to keep it going.

They fixed food and the other men came in one by one. Again, the women served us the food.

After eating, the leader said, "Some of the young boys want to know if Kokopelli would want to stay at least until the snow stops in the spring. They want you to teach them how to make flutes and how to play them," He said. "Not only that but the trails out of here are very difficult to cross now. There is too much snow. Here you will have all you need to eat and can stay as warm as you want to be, like in the south," He added.

"I thank you for such a generous invitation, I accept, I would be crazy to refuse and freeze out in the mountains."

"Then it is settled," the leader said, "We will find you a more suitable place to sleep and teach."

I remained the rest of the winter with them, and I did indeed have everything I wanted; the cooks and Agua Dulce saw to that. In the spring when the first buds grew out of the trees, I told them I must leave. They told me if I ever wanted to return they would be there waiting. They had been in the same place for many seasons and would never leave.

The morning I left all the people, I had been close to gathered to see me off. One of the young men put the ladder down for me to leave. Agua Dulce followed me down and was the last one to say adios to me.

She whispered that she hoped some sun in the future I would return to see my child. I looked at her startled, I had no idea she would be having my child. I looked down at her stomach and she was starting to swell around the middle. I stood there before her uncertain as to what to do.

She took my arm, and turned me to face the trail and gave me a gentle shove in its direction, telling me to go, because I had things to do. Once again, I was leaving people that I had grown to love. However, I had things to do and people to meet and teach. I had my mission. That did not make it any easier; I felt tears well up in my eyes and a thick lump in my throat. I kept on walking - not looking back.

The elders told me the best way to get to lower country was to follow the mountains that went to the south and east. I walked for many suns through hard and difficult country. I walked until Grandfather Sun was directly over my head. As I entered a beautiful valley, ahead of me, I could see a small cluster of dwellings (Taos Pueblo).

As I got closer, people came out to meet me. I walked with them to the center of the village. They asked me to sit and eat as if they knew I was coming. They were very friendly people. They wanted to know if I had any stories to tell them. I told them about the people I left recently and how well I was treated. One of the elders said they knew of the Anasazi and heard of Kokopelli. Word had reached them from the south, that I was coming their way.

I played my flute for them. Everyone seemed to enjoy it. I suppose, it was that I brought something different into their lives. They wanted to know if I would stay with them for a few suns. I declined their offer and I did not even know why. However, I felt an urgency to keep going.

I went on after I had eaten and rested. I was still walking south and east, following a faint trail that climbed sharply into some very steep crags. I began to think I had taken the wrong trail. Something just kept pushing me forward.

CHAPTER 19

THE JOURNEY HOME

I woke up again. I looked about me and could see very little. Why has no one come to help me? I asked the windy cloudy sky. The only answer I got was the wind whistling through the sage.

I felt so lonely, laying here by myself. I thought of all the people I have met and known and now find myself lying here alone. I feel tears form in my eyes. As they overflow my eyelids, they roll down my cheeks and I feel them freeze before they fall. The wind is suddenly much colder. I think to myself, if I am not found soon, I might not survive the night. No, I tell myself, one of my friends will come and save me.

"Where are all my friends now when I need them the most?" I yell feebly at the sky and God. There is no answer.

I try to move again and cannot. My arms and legs have lost all feeling. I look to the heavens and ask the Creator why he does not come and help. I have my eyes open but it seems to be getting darker. Again, I ask why has everyone abandoned me when I tried so hard to help others?

Suddenly through the darkness of my eyes, I see a mist forming in front of me. It is my old friend, the man from the beach. Finally, I think, someone has heard me and come to help.

"I have come to help you," the old man said whispering. "Your work here is finished and you have done it well. You asked me my name before and I told you it was not important. Now I think you must know who I am. I am God, the one you always pray to. Come with me, the moment has come for you to return home."

I cry to him, "I do not want to go, I am not ready."

He does not listen to me. He starts rising and beckons for me to follow.

"How can I follow you when I cannot even move?"

Then I feel myself rising toward him. I dread falling, but feel no more pain and no more cold. I keep going up. I turn and look at my broken and bleeding body, still lying on the ground and feel afraid of falling again. I look at him as he ascends.

Though I wanted to return to my body, the place I was going with him, was filled with warmth, kindness, and beauty. It felt so comfortable and peaceful, that I started to reconsider going back. The lack of pain, cold, and discomfort convinced me to finally let go. Silently I thanked the Creator for taking me home.

Resigned to my fate, I look back at my body once more, and it is gone.

THE END

ABOUT THE AUTHOR

Manny Twofeathers, Aztec and Yaqui, was born in Arizona. He was largely influenced by the southwest legends and native spirituality born of his ancestry. He has authored 2 hugely successful books: "My Road to the Sundance" (published by Hyperion and 2002 edition by Wo-Pila Publishing) and "Stone People Medicine" (published by Wo-Pila Publishing and New World Library) – both lean toward native spirituality, and have been published in foreign languages. Twofeathers is a spiritual elder and counselor. He travels extensively performing spiritual ceremonies, giving lectures and workshops throughout the U.S., Canada and Europe. He currently lives in Pennsylvania with his wife and their 2 children.

If you cannot find this book in your local bookstore or library, call:

814-868-5331

Or write: Wo-Pila Publishing, P.O. Box 8966
Erie, PA. 16505-0966

Website: www.MannyTwofeathers.com
Email: MannyTwofeathers@aol.com

Also look for Manny Twofeathers' other books:

My Road to the Sundance: My Vision Continues
Wo-Pila Publishing, 2002 edition
ISBN: 1-886340-18-8

Stone People Medicine: A Native American Oracle
New World Library Publishing, Novato, CA.
ISBN: 1-57731137X Boxed, with cards and book

We also have available many native arts and crafts by the author and his family. These include the Stone People Medicine, featuring Kokopelli; Dream Catchers, Medicine Wheels, Spirit Crystals, etc. for retail and wholesale.
Please call for more information.